HUMANITY

MARTIN TUFFS

Published by Martin Tuffs

ISBN: 978-1-3999-6691-7

To my Family

past, present and future

AUTHOR'S NOTE

For reasons of inclusivity and in an effort to be dyslexic-friendly, I have gone against industry standards and used a sans-serif font (Calibri) with the text aligned to the left without justification.

I hope you enjoy the read.

Martin Tuffs 2023

ACKNOWLEDGMENTS

Thanks to my wife, Andrea, for her patience while I write away almost every day, even on holiday, on my various devices. To my children who never fail to provide me with ideas. And to my parents who have offered continuous encouragement while I was writing. Thanks also to my colleagues from over the years who I count as friends. Thanks to the dedicated staff at Nottingham University Hospitals and my local surgery for getting me back to health after bowel cancer. Thanks to all of you for the inspiration. And, of course, thanks to you, the reader, for taking a look at my story.

Dear guest,

I hope you enjoy the read.

fellow passenger on the 'Spirit of ~~Adventure~~ 🙂 Discovery''

Matt Yates

Sept 25

Norway

CHAPTER ONE

Standing by the barrier, waiting for the train to pass summed up my day, my week, my life. Whenever I was strongly minded to do something, obstacles would soon appear, frustrating my progress and holding me back. In this case, I was anxious to get home as a storm was fast approaching, and as I reached the crossing, the barriers came down. With red flashing lights warning of an oncoming train, I found myself gazing at the pedestrian gate in front of me. A sign cautioned against crossing when the barriers were down, but should I take the chance? There would be plenty of time for me to get across as the train had not yet come into sight. But I played it safe, obeying the rules, like normal, and waited.

Having been cooped up in the office all day, the mildness of the autumn evening had lured me out. I had felt the need to stretch my legs but, more particularly, to fill my lungs with air and destress. I had taken my usual route over the crossing and down a quiet, tree-lined lane, just off the main road which took me past St Mary's that stood among blackened gravestones. The church was built on the high ground of a gravel ridge and behind it was the local nature reserve. I had walked a circuit of the lake, a remnant of the gravel pit that had long since been quarried, without meeting a soul and headed for home. As I walked back past the church, the solitary lamp that adorned the wooden lychgate lit up in front of me. As I could not see a motion detector, I surmised that the light coming on as I approached was a mere coincidence, perhaps activated by the onset of dusk. I had instinctively paused and looked up to see dark, leaden clouds drifting in from the west, a sure sign that rain was on its way. I felt the chill air of a sudden breeze and the hairs on the back of my neck bristled. I had zipped up my hoody, set off with a quickened pace and was soon back on the main road only to come up against the barrier.

A minute or so went by before the train appeared, passing slowly in front of me as it prepared to stop at the station just beyond the crossing. As I tried to resolve individual faces from the shadowy silhouettes of passengers through the carriage windows, there was an explosion of light accompanied by a thunderous crack, and I was launched into the air amidst a cloud of dust.

A dead silence ensued and, to my astonishment, I found myself sitting in the road and looking back towards the crossing. I had been thrown a good ten yards and felt lightheaded but otherwise unscathed. As I came back to myself, the barriers rose and a lady, who was dressed in jogging gear and had been waiting at the other side, sprinted over the crossing and dropped to her knees. To my horror, I realised she was attending a body that was lying face down in the road, I froze.

"Quick, phone an ambulance," she shouted in my direction, "the lightning strike has knocked him unconscious."

Fumbling around in my pockets to find my phone, I realised all feeling in my hands had been lost, perhaps I had sustained injuries after all. Raising my hands to my face, I could see nothing remarkable about them. As I got to my feet, legs weightless with trepidation, a man brushed passed me.

"I'm on it," he shouted back to the lady and rushed to join her. He gave brief details to the emergency services before looking toward the lady for advice.

"Tell them he's alive but unconscious," she instructed, "his breathing is okay and I've not had to do CPR but he's been out for about a minute."

I found myself faltering towards the scene, was I that terrified of what I might find? The lady began to gently roll the victim onto his side. I realised that this would reveal his face, and I braced myself for whatever injuries had been sustained. A moment later, I froze once again, this time in sheer terror, I recognised the face, it was mine. Enduring a blast of horror, the only thought I could muster was would I survive?

"Will he be okay?" I asked, staring at the lady, but she gave me no response. Perhaps, she hadn't heard, with the gusting wind and the train now revving as it pulled out of the station. I asked again, this time shouting above the background noise. "Will he be okay?" Still no response.

I looked around, a middle-aged lady, under the cover of a raincoat, ran from the end terrace house nearest the station to assist and was soon dispatched to get some blankets. I looked at the ground to see it soaking wet, it was pouring down. How was I not feeling the rain, or the cold for that matter?

“Can anyone see me?” I yelled, yet still no response. The conclusion was inevitable; I was totally invisible to my clutch of helpers. My thoughts began to crystalise, was I having an out-of-body experience? But everything seemed so vivid and detailed: I could read every word on the crossing warning sign, resolve every brick in the gable of the end terrace house and see the train disappearing into the distance. Then again, I had used the crossing hundreds of times and the whole area was very familiar to me. Perhaps, in a state of insensibility, my memory had constructed the scenery and, upon hearing voices, my imagination was doing the rest. All this hung together, sort of, until the lady spoke again.

“He’s coming to,” she said, as the older lady returned with blankets that they placed around my waking body.

“That’s time up,” I thought, “well, this will give me a great story to tell Lou, not that she will believe me.”

And I stood expecting to re-emerge inside my skin.

“Can you hear me?” said the lady.

“Yeah,” came the reply from my body.

“What’s your name?”

“Fred.” My body paused before adding, “Plain old Fred.” This was how I had taken to introducing myself of late and which reflected the melancholia that had settled upon me over the last few months.

“Stay still Fred, help is on its way.”

“What happened?”

“Lightning struck the ground right in front of you just as the train was passing. You’re lucky it didn’t hit you directly, it’s made a bit of a mess of the road. You lost consciousness and have a cut on your forehead from where you hit the ground. How do you feel?"

"Shaky and cold."

"I'm not surprised, that will be shock."

I listened in complete confusion. Why was I not back inside my skin? As far as I knew, to have an out-of-body experience then you had to be at least unconscious.

"Trust me to be different," I muttered as I knelt to address myself. "Can you see me?" As I had anticipated, there was no response.

Convincing myself the whole ridiculous episode was a result of shock as the lady said, I stood up and took stock, perhaps it was akin to having double vision after a knock to the head and things would settle down in good time. I watched as my three helpers stood guard over me, the gentleman guiding the odd car around the scene until the ambulance arrived.

The two paramedics spent several minutes examining my body and questioning the lady, who they thanked, telling her she had done the right things. The conclusion was that an assessment at the hospital was needed, among other concerns they were worried about my heart. As the lady paramedic guided my body into the ambulance and sat him up on the bed, my overriding instinct was to follow. After we had set off and with my body looking comfortable, I started to wonder about the possibilities of my state, could I pass through walls or even float as if a ghostly apparition? I started to experiment and found that the side of the ambulance stopped my hand as if I was flesh and blood. I made a small jump and gravity brought me back down as if I was in my earthly body. My hands were still completely numb, as was the rest of me. Experimenting further, I found that I could not pick up the slightest thing: not the blanket on the bed, not a pen on the medic's tray and not even a wafer-thin tissue poking from its box. In short, although I could still think and move at will, I could affect nothing, I was a mere spectator.

Once inside the hospital, my body was handed over to a member of staff, dressed in pale blue scrubs, who asked if there was anyone that he would like to contact. This prompted my body to call Lou from his mobile and for which I was very grateful, she would have already started to worry about my failure to return home.

Lou was introduced to me by a mutual friend when I was looking for new accommodation, about a year back, as he knew Lou had recently moved onto the property ladder and was looking for a lodger. Being of similar ages and backgrounds, Lou and I immediately hit it off and I moved in three weeks later. Lou was pleased with the arrangement as it helped pay the bills and gave her company. I was equally pleased as the house was comfortable, her conversation amusing and it gave me company too, company which I had never tired of. Lou was a drama teacher at an academy close to the city centre and, with my office only a five-minute walk from her school, I hitched a lift with her every morning.

Finishing work much later than Lou, I relied on the tram to get home, a stop was right outside the office and the terminus not far from Lou's house. Lou was a passionate teacher, often marking books or working on scripts for the latest school play deep into the evening. Our senses of humour were such that we had taken to playing small practical jokes on each other. In my latest prank, I had planted a fake fixed penalty notice on the windscreen of her car after she had been forced by roadworks to park away from the house. Lou discovered the false ticket when we were leaving for work and had become uncharacteristically upset with tears welling in her eyes. Her distress made me regret my actions immediately; I admitted the ticket was my doing and apologised repeatedly. Lou had vowed revenge and I was feeling more than a little apprehensive about what that might be.

The call to Lou was not straightforward as, at first, she took his news to be a joke, something that my body did not take kindly to, his abruptness and raised voice unnerved me. However, Lou made allowances and, in her typical fashion, offered to come straight to the hospital. My body's mood lightened and they agreed that she should hold off until he had been seen by a doctor, an overnight stay was already on the horizon.

After the call, my mind turned back to the absurd situation; how was my body continuing without me? Had I suffered a complete nervous breakdown and was I literally out of my mind? Would the staff spot something amiss and would they be able to cure me? Question after question emerged from my web of thoughts, all innocuous until I reached the shadows of my mind. Were dark, unearthly forces at work? Was I my soul, which was now at stake being away from the protection of my body? Was the lamp coming on in the lychgate a sinister omen? I had no answers, and my nerve, which had so far been held together by the novelty of the circumstances, was unfolding rapidly. I urged myself to put my faith in medical science and not to think of anything beyond humanity.

After a wait of around fifteen minutes, my body was guided to a side room by a consulting doctor. She was full of enthusiasm despite the lateness of the hour and after a short preamble began her examination. First, she held a stethoscope to his chest and then shone a light into each of his eyes. With a concerned smile, she started to get to the crux of the matter.

"How do you feel?" she asked.

"Fine, a little shaky still, when will I be discharged?" my body replied.

"When we've taken a good look at you. How is your vision?"

"Fine."

"Any blurring?"

"No."

"Are you sure? You seem to be blinking a lot."

"I'm fine."

"Hmm. How many fingers?"

"Three."

"What year is it?"

"Twenty twenty-two"

"What day is it?"

"Friday."

"What time is it?"

"It's time I went home."

I did not think the remark, or the sarcastic way in which my body had delivered it, was appropriate, and neither did the doctor.

"Hmm."

"About half seven."

My body's answers seemed broadly satisfactory, minus the sarcasm, though the doctor looked at him with narrowing eyes and persisted with questions about mental awareness, she seemed to have recognised something was not quite right. It appeared to me that my body had started to become uncooperative, uncharacteristic for me, and more focused on getting home than anything else. The doctor's concluding opinion, however, was that he should be admitted for further assessment and an ECG of the heart was needed before release.

Within half an hour my body was escorted to a third-floor ward by a porter. We passed through a secured door and along a corridor with rooms of six beds, three on each side, branching off at intervals. When we reached the third room, a nurse took over, guiding my body to a bed and issuing him with a hospital gown, thick treaded socks, a plastic glass and a jug of water. The other five beds were occupied by older gentlemen, who watched with scrutiny as the nurse gave my body a debrief on the hospital's routine, which my body barely listened to.

With the admission procedures over, the nurse returned to his desk and diligently set about some paperwork. The gentleman in the next bed attempted to engage in small talk but my body's lack of interest ensured that the conversation soon fizzled out. As a quiet fell over the ward, my body took up residence in the bedside chair and became engrossed in his phone.

Posting myself at the foot of the bed, I started to analyse my state. I was not hungry, nor thirsty. In fact, I had no compulsion for the ins and outs of the human body at all. I did have emotions, an abundance of them, most of them negative. I felt worried, wary and anxious. Above all, I felt a deep sense of loneliness, the loneliness of a cautious new arrival in a crowded city. No one to talk to and no one to listen to, at least not in any meaningful way. A reprioritisation had taken place, I was not feeling the urge to check my phone for the breaking news or latest sports results, not that I could do that. I was, however, longing to talk to Lou. How she would laugh when I came out of this concussion, or whatever it was, and I told her of my out-of-body experience. I thought about how I should collect some verifiable evidence to prove that it was not a joke on my part. Surely, I would wake up from my torment soon and normality would return.

My body broke the ward silence.

"Any tea?" he bellowed across to the nurse who looked up in only mild annoyance, probably wondering if the question was an attempt at humour on my body's part. The nurse played it straight.

"The drinks trolley comes round at nine o'clock tomorrow morning, there will be tea, coffee, milk and orange juice."

"Hmph."

"There's a machine in the cafe near the entrance if you want to walk down."

"Hmph, can't you go for me?"

"I can't leave my station."

The silence returned only for my body to break it a few minutes later.

"My battery's going flat, anyone got a phone charger?" My body was now engaging the rest of the ward and scanning from one patient to another. His question only returned a few murmurs and shakes of heads. "Hmph thought so," he added before muttering under his breath, "what did I expect from a bunch of old codgers?"

The nurse appeared.

"Here, you can borrow mine," he said.

My body took the charger without saying thank you. I

despaired; my body's attitude was deeply unnerving. I needed to try and take back control before he caused any real damage. A thought occurred to me, could I simply merge back into my body? As he stood and turned to the wall to plug the charger into the socket, I took my chance. I sidled up to him, braced myself and took a step forward. As I made contact, I felt a repelling force, like opposing magnets, and was pushed back. I tried again but with the same result. So, I was stuck on the outside with no obvious way back.

Without the distraction of his phone, my body began to doze in the chair, his eyes looked sallow and drawn. I wondered if his mind was in the same bewildered state as mine or if he was even aware of the displacement that had taken place. Soon after the ward lights were dimmed, my body got up from the bedside chair, changed into his gown and was soon beneath the pastel blue blankets. I took up residence in the newly vacated chair and tried to make sense of what had happened to me, and what was still happening to me, but my thoughts were disconnected, muddled and confused. I looked across at my body who was drifting off to sleep and I too felt myself slipping away into unconsciousness. Was this to be the end of my ordeal? Would I wake to find myself back in my body? Had it all been a dream? These were my final thoughts before the darkness and quiet of a deep sleep overcame me.

CHAPTER TWO

I awoke just after seven o'clock, still in the bedside chair, and turned to see my body with a thermometer hanging from his bottom lip. I sighed, there had been no return to my body and my physical state was just as it had been the night before. I was still unseen and still unheard. In the ward, the morning health checks were in progress and my body did not look pleased about the timings. The nurse, her face set in a sympathetic stare, retrieved the thermometer and then wrapped the blood pressure monitor sleeve around his arm.

"You may feel a tightening," she said in reassurance, as the sleeve began to inflate.

"I know how a blood pressure monitor works," replied my body in a flat, antagonistic tone. His attitude had not improved with the benefit of a night's rest.

"Were you admitted last night?"

"Yes."

An uncomfortable silence ensued which lasted until the nurse had finished the checks.

"All normal," she offered as if the news might encourage a few friendly words.

"Thought so," returned my body bluntly. I groaned.

The nurse glanced at the jug full of water on the overbed table.

"And Fred, remember to keep your fluid levels up." As she turned to attend to the next patient, my body glared at her with menacing pinpoint pupils. I was not impressed; my natural habit was affability but the behaviour of my body verged on abusive, made worse by the fact his discourtesy was aimed at the very people who were looking after him. I sat back trying once again to figure out what was happening.

My thinking was clearer than it had been the previous evening and thoughts that I was in some sort of weird dream were fading. Was I truly having an out-of-body experience? But how? Had the lightning literally blasted me from my shell? My thoughts returned to the occult. Was I indeed a soul that had left the protective shield of its body? Was my body without virtue and was that why he was so disagreeable? Would his behaviour deteriorate further? His stare at the nurse had unsettled me. How would he behave with Lou? Would he destroy our friendship? I needed help. I remembered a sign to the multi-faith prayer room on my way to the ward, perhaps, such a place of sanctity would provide some much-needed solace, so I set off following one of the medical staff out through the ward doors.

Walking along the hospital corridors was exhausting with the bobbing and weaving of people heading towards each other. Some meandered into my path, others jinked into it at the last moment but all delivered me a judder as I felt human contact, yet they seemed to feel nothing or so little that it did not register. I constantly scanned the eyes of those approaching, half in the hope they might see me but none did.

The prayer room was on a branch off the main corridor. The notice outside showed symbols of twelve religions, and with so many faiths represented I opened my mind; comfort from any direction would be welcome. The door was ajar, it seemed as if there were to be no barriers here at least, and I passed through to find the place unoccupied. It was a bright, uncluttered room with clean white walls, a mauve carpet and a low-hanging ceiling. There were no overt signs of any particular religion save a solitary candle flickering orange on a wooden plinth table. As the flame gently changed colour from orange to yellow then green, I realised it was electronic and watched as the colours continued to cycle through those of the rainbow. There was a large abstract painted on the front wall, shards of blue, gold and white bursting from a bright central point, all the brighter courtesy of the strategically placed spotlights above. A single line of cushioned chairs faced the abstract, and I took a seat in the middle of the row. Staring at the image, it came to me that I was looking at a portrayal of an angel with great golden wings spread on either side of a central body. The revelation gave me a focal point and, to my surprise, I found myself silently asking for help, praying to the blessed angel to bring my unnerving experience to a positive conclusion.

Absorbing the tranquillity, I sat for several minutes in the sanctity of the room and appreciated the mural. As I stared, more detail of the angel revealed itself, I could make out a head thrown back as if looking towards heaven and golden hair flowing around her shoulders.

What at first sight had seemed to be a blur of colour was now taking quite a different form, it was captivating. Having revealed all the detail that I thought I could, I quietly left and soon found myself back in the main corridor. With the morning business of the hospital underway, I found staff, patients and visitors all walking blindly by me, and the loneliness of my situation seemed tenfold until one particular individual caught my eye. She stood out among all the other passers-by due to her bright smile. She was dressed in an unfastened yellow coat, a loose-fitting white top, cream cropped trousers and white canvas boots. As she approached, her happy expression brought a curious smile to my face, her gaze turned in my direction and it appeared she was looking directly at me.

"Hi, I'm Fang?" she said. I was astonished and her introduction had brought me to an absolute standstill. I managed to blurt out a response.

"You can see me?"

"Sure, I can see you." With a hundred thoughts fogging my mind, I was stunned and found myself not knowing what to say next. I wondered if I was somehow back to normal, that I had reappeared. As we stood facing each other, a porter rushing by caused us both to jump back, the implication was clear. "But no one else can see you?" she added. Her tone was calm, natural even, as if a state of invisibility was something she was accustomed to.

"That's right, not even myself can see me."

"Yourself?"

"Yeah, my body is upstairs recovering from a lightning strike, I seem to be having an out-of-body experience, I know that sounds totally weird by the way." With my tongue unlocked, I briefly described what had happened at the crossing. My new acquaintance stared at me with widened eyes.

"Yesterday, it would have sounded weird. Today, I believe every word you've said because the same has happened to me. I thought I might be dreaming the whole thing but you look real."

"I am real, at least, if it's anybody's dream then it's mine."

She was now looking directly into my eyes as if evaluating me. I had to glance away, looking people in the eyes was not my strong point. Realising that turning away had probably made me look furtive, I looked back again and this time her smile drew my gaze to the centre of her face. Her features were mesmerising, and I took the glimmering light that shone across her nose and cheeks as her natural state of fluorescence, stood before me was a real person. With my thoughts settling, I was becoming more and more curious about my new acquaintance who seemed to be unfazed by an experience that must have been as traumatic as mine. She took a step back and looked me up and down. I felt a little self-conscious in my market stall chinos, faded navy hoody and worn-away trainers.

"Do you know what?" she said with her smile broadening. "I definitely think you are real." I was glad to hear it but so brimming with curiosity that I neglected to introduce myself. Instead, I let loose with questions.

"What happened to you, I mean, how did you leave your body?"

"Where to start?" She paused momentarily, scrunching her lips as if an ordering of thoughts was taking place, then ushered me to the side of the corridor to avoid the stream of passers-by. "The thing is, I only arrived in the UK from Singapore yesterday. Having travelled across London from the airport, I caught the train to Nottingham from St Pancras. I'd not been able to sleep on the plane, and it wasn't long after leaving London that I dozed off. I woke with fright to find myself sprawled on the floor of the aisle. I thought there must have been a crash and I'd been thrown from my seat but the train was running smoothly and the few people left in the carriage were sitting as if nothing had happened. The next thing, we stopped at a station. Are you still with me?"

"Perfectly." I softened my expression, sensing my hard stare, which was my custom when listening with great concentration, might have been off-putting. With the break in conversation came another of my questions. "Do you remember the station name?"

"I didn't notice though what I do remember is a feeling of confusion; why was I on the floor and why was no one coming to help? As the train started to move again, I pulled myself up to realise that I was completely numb from head to toe; whatever had happened had robbed me of my sense of touch. A lady was sitting in one of the window seats tapping furiously on her phone, I asked if she'd seen what had happened but she could neither see nor hear me. My seat was a few rows away so I walked back to find that my place was already taken - by me. Now, I was really scared.

"I tried to shake my body's shoulder, to wake her but my hand was pushed away. I walked down the carriage to find no one could see or hear me so just sat opposite my body trying to figure out what was going on. As we pulled into Nottingham, the lady with the phone moved down the carriage and seeing my body asleep, tapped her on the shoulder. This time, my body woke though she couldn't sense me. The lady said that they had arrived in Nottingham, the train's final destination. My body quickly stood to collect her luggage from the overhead rack but came over faint and had to sit back down. The lady started to take a greater interest and said that lightning had struck right outside the window where my body was sat, just two stops down the line, and there might have been some effect."

I had listened intently, gripped by the unfolding story that in so many ways mirrored mine, but one detail meant that my curiosity was brimming over once again.

"Two stops before Nottingham, that's where I was struck. The crossing I spoke about is at the end of the station platform, that's where I was waiting to cross. What time did it happen, the strike, I mean?"

"The train was due to arrive in Nottingham at five past six, it was about ten minutes before then. I checked my smartwatch but it's not so smart anymore, look." And she held out the black screen, tapping it to show there was no response. "See, kaput."

I looked at the face of my analogue watch and held it up so my new companion could see, it had stopped at exactly five to six.

"Then we were separated from our bodies at the same time and place, it was your train that passed in front of me just as the lightning struck." I paused; the conclusion seemed obvious but I couldn't reconcile the fact that we'd both been affected. "Do you think it was the lightning that threw us from our bodies?" My new acquaintance peered at me beneath raised eyebrows, her answer was yes.

“Ironic really, all the lightning we get in Singapore and I survive unscathed for twenty-two years; I am in the UK for less than five hours and this happens.”

“And where’s your body now?”

“That’s the thing, I’m trying to find her. On leaving the train, she started to shake and complained of blurred vision. The lady was so concerned that she insisted on taking my body to the emergency department of the nearby hospital. I followed them to the station car park but was not able to get in the car and watched helplessly as they drove off. I followed in their direction and then picked up on signs to the hospital. It didn’t take long to find the emergency department but there was no trace of my body or the lady. I checked out other parts of the hospital but started feeling sleepy so found a seat in a quiet corner to rest. Next thing, I’m waking up and still in the hospital. I decided that it’s probable that my body is already at the hotel, I forget the exact address so thought, if nothing else happens, I’ll head towards the city to look for it. Now something has happened, you.”

If my plight was bad, hers seemed worse; I felt compelled to help.

“Did you say your name was Fang?”

“That’s right.”

Inwardly, I heaved a sigh of relief, I was in the habit of misremembering people’s names, something which had led to much dismay in the past.

“Hey, that’s a great name, by the way, mine’s plain old Fred.”

“That’s an unusual name, Plain Old Fred.”

“No, just Fred, I guess I was trying to say that my name seems quite plain.”

“I know, I was trying out humour, I heard it’s a good

way to make friends here. Isn't comedy the cultural currency of the UK?" I laughed politely and was already admiring Fang's astuteness.

"Cultural currency, I've never thought about it like that, there's probably something in it though."

"Isn't that another trait of the British, self-depreciation, the way you called your name plain."

"Generally speaking, that's true. What else do you know about the Brits?"

"That you're polite, like to help, talk in idioms, 'beat around the bush' and don't know how to end a conversation." I laughed again, this time for real, though I wasn't sure if Fang had meant to be humourous or not. In any case, she had given me the perfect opportunity to offer assistance.

"That's an excellent thumbnail sketch of us, and funnily enough I was about to ask if you would like help in finding your hotel."

"That would be great, it's called the Mercury."

The Mercury was a hotel that we recommended at work to visitors, who very often returned glowing accounts of the service and the individuality of the rooms. It was popular with tourists and business types alike with its central location and a touch of opulence that set it apart from the many chain hotels scattered around the city centre. As far as I knew, the Mercury was independently owned and, with only forty or so rooms, was able to give guests a personal touch.

"I know it, it's not much more than a mile from here. I could escort you there if you like?"

"I'd be very grateful, thank you." As she spoke, Fang put her hands together to reinforce her gratitude. I smiled in nervous excitement, pleased at the thought of spending time with my new companion and it felt like I should be the one giving thanks.

"I've just had an idea, why don't we go to the ward where my body is? There were two rooms with female patients and, perhaps, if your body was admitted she's there, if she isn't then we'll go straight to the hotel. We could catch a bus from outside the hospital."

"Perfect."

As Fang and I chatted on the way to the ward, we discovered many parallels: our appearances were exactly as they had been when the lightning struck, neither of us could affect our surroundings, we had no physical feelings and we had both felt the instinctive need to follow our bodies hoping we would somehow re-join. As we continued to swap details of the fateful night, Fang described her horror when the lady drove off with her body. I began to worry, did the lady really take her body to the hospital? Or were her motives far less charitable? Thinking back, I had not seen Fang's body during my time in the emergency department, surely our visits would have coincided. Then where did the lady take Fang's body? My negative bias was kicking in again and I steeled myself to concentrate on helping. I would say nothing of my concerns to Fang.

CHAPTER THREE

We found the ward door to be closed so began to wait until someone entered or left so we could gain entry. Fang looked towards the side of the door; I followed her gaze and saw a small notice stating 'Press for Attention.' Fang duly pressed the sensor beneath the notice, silence.

"You try," Fang suggested. I obliged to silence once again. "Try again."

I tried again and this time, as my finger reached the sensor, Fang's finger joined mine and a buzzer sounded. We looked at each other with amazement; had we caused the reaction? We touched the sensor together again and once again a buzzer sounded. We had discovered a way to affect our surroundings. As we mused, a nurse opened the door and, seeing no one, looked down the corridor with crossed eyebrows.

"Playing knicky knocky ido in a hospital, disgraceful," she muttered before withdrawing back into the confines of the ward.

As we slipped through the closing door, Fang turned

to me with a look of puzzlement.

"What's knicky knocky ido?"

"It's a street game," I replied, "you knock on someone's door, or ring their doorbell, then run off and hide somewhere to watch as they answer their door."

"And that's a game?"

"Well, it's more of a prank than a game, I guess. It's tolerated if children are the perpetrators." I sensed Fang was amused by my explanation so added more, determined to be light-hearted, her smile was a tonic. "Different parts of the country call it different things. I'm from the North and call it knicky knocky ido. I suspect the nurse is northern too. They call it knocka door run in the Midlands and knock knock ginger in the South."

"How do you know all this?"

"Well, I suppose as I've met people from other parts of the country, the game occasionally crops up in casual conversation and you discover this difference in terminology between regions. You might already know about the number of terms we have for a bread roll here."

"That's right, and I read about the dialects you have throughout your country."

"Did you know that humour varies throughout the regions as well?" I turned to Fang with a deadpan expression. "If I tell a joke in Nottingham, they won't get it in London."

"Why not?"

"They won't hear it."

It was now Fang who laughed for real. I was not in the habit of telling jokes, I struggled to remember them, though was glad I had remembered this one for the broadest of smiles was spread across Fang's face and I found my loneliness melting away. There was a familiar air about Fang, perhaps it was that she had so easily adopted the British habit of making light in the direst of circumstances. She had already had a positive effect on my mood; I was starting to feel optimistic and with her by my side, our predicament was beginning to feel like an adventure.

In the ward, there was no sign of Fang's body so we took the chance to check up on mine. To my discomfort, he was complaining about the tea which, according to him, was stewed and undrinkable. He caught the attention of the drinks trolley attendant, who had only made it to the next bed, and demanded a coffee instead. The rest of the ward looked on in disquiet. I apologised to Fang for my body's ill-mannered behaviour and with that, we left for the hotel.

At the front of the hospital, there was a row of bus shelters together with a large digital screen that helpfully displayed the destination, routes and times of the most imminent arrivals. This essential information was alternated with adverts for nearby venues and attractions. Under a sullen sky, the details on the screen were easily read and I soon found the number of the bus we needed. We joined the disorderly queue, mainly hospital staff coming off shift, I presumed.

"When the bus arrives, in two minutes according to the screen, we'll get ahead of these people to make sure we can get on," I said, before adding a cautionary note. "Never queue jump in Britain when your back inside your body though, you'll never be forgiven, it would be like stealing ice cream off a child."

"Don't worry," replied Fang, "it's the same in Singapore and you know what? I think I'm going to like it here."

Our bus arrived, silently drawing up to the kerb. It was the electric type of the most modern design and looked brand new. I felt a tinge of pride that Fang's first bus journey in the UK would be on a vehicle with such obvious environmental credentials. We took up position in a pair of seats close to the front. Looking back at the hospital, I was reminded of its vastness with two huge five-story square blocks on either side of a wide canopied entrance and wondered about the thousands of human stories contained within. The bus quietly pulled off and sped down through a tunnel, cut into the sandstone ridge that marked the west side of the hospital grounds, to emerge on the main road on the other side.

The journey was only a few minutes, and I pointed out the odd building of interest as we went. With the hotel almost in sight, I suggested that we should start making our way to the front of the bus. As we got up to move, Fang noticed a stop button on the rail next to her seat and turned to meet my gaze.

"Let's try," she said with her eyes beaming, "as an experiment." As we placed our fingers at the centre of the button, a bleeping noise rang out and the 'stopping' sign at the front of the bus illuminated.

"I don't believe that," I remarked and started to examine the button. It looked different to the traditional red ones that I was familiar with from less modern buses, perhaps, the mechanism was ultrasensitive or driven by a sensor like the ward door. With no time to ponder, we made our way to the very front of the bus and, as the doors opened, jumped off. Looking back, it occurred to me that someone could have pressed a button elsewhere on the bus and that such an occurrence would explain the bleeper being set off. However, no one else had moved from their seats, something that had not gone unnoticed by the driver who was peering into his rear-view mirror.

"Is anyone getting off?" he bellowed, turning around to connect with his audience. He muttered something under his breath before adding. "Did anyone press the button?" Having received no response, other than bemused looks, he shook his head, closed the doors and drove off. I looked towards Fang with a sheepish grin. Fang looked far from sheepish, in fact, she looked positively pleased and span around on her toes.

"Knicky knocky ido," she said triumphantly while giving me a sideways glance, then tried and failed to suppress her laughter. My heart warmed.

CHAPTER FOUR

The Mercury Hotel was a red sandstone Georgian building which stood proudly on a busy corner in Nottingham's theatrical quarter. The neat white framed sash windows cascaded up to the fourth story with the fifth comprised of dormers protruding from a grey slated roof. As a guest left through the large glass doors at the entrance, Fang and I whisked past and found ourselves in a spacious lobby.

We made our way over to the reception. The counter gate, which allowed staff from behind out into the lobby, was open. The receptionist, Ivor according to his name badge, donned a smart burgundy jacket with black lapels and was busy with an elderly couple at the tourist information stand, which stood just to the right of the reception and alongside a vending machine. A banner across the information stand, which was bristling with leaflets, announced 'Find your local attraction.'

Fang led as we made our way behind the counter and then through an open door that revealed a small office.

As I hesitated in the doorway, she stepped in and looked around. Anxiety had settled upon me. Crammed in the room were two desks, facing each other, both adorned with desktop computers. There were no windows and the wall space was taken with charts and calendars. Fang moved from one computer to the other, then scrutinised some paperwork left out on one of the desks. As she lingered, my anxiety grew, and I realised why, it was the fear of an enclosed space, the fear that the door could be shut and we would be trapped. Furthermore, I was becoming paranoid that we could somehow reappear and be caught snooping around. Fang seemed to have no such qualms.

"Fang, what are you doing?" I said, hoping to hurry her along.

"Just looking to see if there is any sign that my body has checked in but there's nothing. Let's see if there's anything at the front."

Under the line of the front counter was a desk with a laptop. The screen displayed a full page of text and as Fang scanned down, Ivor returned through the counter gate, closed the flap and walked across to the laptop. We jumped back, Fang looked at me and shook her head, I took this to mean she had found no record of her body. Ivor tapped away on the keyboard as the old couple joined him on the other side of the counter.

"That's you fully booked in," said Ivor. "Someone will bring your cases up soon and if there's anything else let me know."

"We will," said the lady, putting the leaflets that Ivor had picked out into her handbag, "and thanks for taking the time."

"That's all right, only too happy. And besides, it's

been quiet this morning."

"Thanks all the same, and thanks for the leaflets," offered the man, "we might even go to the castle later today."

"You won't regret it, and they've got a nice café that does cream teas for a weekend treat," said Ivor.

"I hear you," responded the man patting his portly midriff, "the diet can wait till Monday."

"Enjoy your day."

"We will. By the way, what time does the restaurant here open this evening?"

I smiled, with the conversation rekindling, Fang's thumbnail sketch of the British was playing out in front of us.

"Let's assume I've checked in," said Fang, spotting a pair of comfy chairs next to a low table. "We'll take a seat over there; it will give us a good view of the lobby. If my body walks through, we'll see her." We dipped below the counter and took up our strategic position.

Our seats gave us a fine view of the hotel entrance, the reception desk, the entrance to the restaurant, the bottom of the staircase and the lifts - all angles covered. It was just gone eleven o'clock with guests and occasional visitors filtering into the restaurant for morning coffee. As we sat back in contemplation, our conversation concentrated on domestic matters. Fang was fascinated by English culture and asked me question after question about where I was from, my family and what my interests were. It felt a little like I was been studied, but I did not mind, I enjoyed the attention.

I told her of my upbringing in a North Eastern town a mile from the sea, how I came to Nottingham to study business and became accustomed to the place. After finishing my course, a friend found me a job, with decent prospects, in the city centre so I stayed local, renting a flat with friends. Then, as my friends moved away, I found myself more comfortable accommodation with Lou. And, I told of Lou, fondly describing our habits and routines.

I told Fang how I worked in an eye-catching, mirrored glass-fronted office block that was directly opposite a tram stop a few minutes from the city centre. Outside the building was an impressive sculpture, a huge piece made from resin to look like granite which depicted two formless adults guiding a formless child along in front of them. I had never been a fan of modern art but this particular installation I liked, even using an image of it as my phone's screen saver.

I told of how the work involved supporting start-up companies in the local area with market research and website design. And how, in the last year, I had become more involved in business management, all in the name of progression. I did not tell Fang that this change had come at a cost, the work was less interesting and more stressful. I was thinking that I might have made a wrong career turn and should have stuck with what I enjoyed.

Neither did I share that I was thinking of leaving as my efforts were not appreciated. I had even looked into a few full-time courses at the local college, a move that was driven by an aspiration for a complete change of career. Not appreciated? It was worse than that, there were bullying forces at work. 'Nurturing and growth' was the company slogan, at least this was what was written at the top of their homepage. In recent times, I had not seen much nurturing and growth for employees.

After sharing a good deal of my history, the urge to

know more about Fang had become overwhelming, but when I asked reciprocal questions, to do with Fang's home life, then she had skilfully redirected the conversation back to me. If I persisted with such a line of questioning then her eyebrows knotted together. I did not dare to ask if there was a reason for her reticence, though I wondered if there was a hidden sadness, if so, it was probably best not to probe. Still, I was intrigued by my new companion and keen to know more about her. I learned to avoid sensitive areas and restricted my enquiries to Singapore in general. Realising that I did not know the purpose of Fang's visit, and as this seemed to be safe ground, I asked. Fang explained that she worked as an IT specialist for a global technology company, that she was here as a problem solver and to learn about the UK operation whose main office was in Nottingham where she was to be based.

Then Fang broke the news that her visit was only for two weeks. I had not even thought that far ahead, and the idea of being alone once more was unsettling. I was comfortable in Fang's presence; she had never felt like a stranger from the moment she had introduced herself. Fang intrigued me, in little over two hours her familiarity had dispelled my loneliness, and I had almost forgotten our predicament. Our conversation in the lobby had avoided our strange plight, the stark news of Fang's departure made me rethink it.

"I'm hoping things will be back to normal in two weeks," I said, "but what if all this is a dream brought on by the trauma of the lightning strike? Perhaps, I'm unconscious, lying in a hospital bed and who knows when I'll come out of it."

"You know what I think, it's not a dream. The

buildings, the roads, the people, everything looks and sounds as it should. Dreams are vague and fluid." Fang glanced around the lobby. "This is definite, look at it." I looked around and had to agree, it was all definite. "And you don't have dreams when you are unconscious. I'm thinking we are truly having out-of-body experiences, not a dreamt experience but one where our consciousnesses have left our bodies."

"Our consciousnesses?"

"Or, if you prefer, our spirits."

I remembered my concern that my very soul was at stake.

"Do you think our bodies have been taken over by some malignant force? I mean, my body's behaviour is deteriorating, if we're not reunited soon then I hate to think of what I'll be going back to."

"Wow, did your body seem that bad?"

"No, but extremely intolerant."

"Well then, and why would a malignant force displace us?" I liked Fang's more optimistic outlook and shrugged my perplexity. "We'll have to find a way back to humanity though, it won't happen by accident."

"And it won't happen by walking into our bodies, at least, I tried this back at the hospital."

"We'll just have to keep our wits about us, the answer might be just around the corner."

Fang's sentence came to an abrupt stop as she sat upright. I followed her gaze to see Fang's body standing in front of the vending machine. A huge wave of relief surged through me, her body was safe and one of my worries had been laid to waste.

We joined Fang's body and stared into the machine as the spiral dispenser turned. The selected chocolate bar moved forward and stopped, teetering on the very edge of its holder. Fang's body looked across at the reception with an expression of irritation.

"This is an all-too-common problem in the UK," I said, "and there's a common solution." With that, I started to bump the side of the machine with my hip, I was not expecting much to happen but thought it was worth a try. Fang, realising what I was trying to do, joined me, and in unison, we bumped the machine five or six times. The chocolate bar stayed where it was. Just as Fang's body started to move towards the reception, Ivor, who had been watching proceedings, swung up the counter lid and hurried round the reception desk to meet her.

"Let me help," he said, and he bumped the machine with his hip as Fang and I had done. This time the chocolate bar dropped.

Fang's body kneeled and retrieved the chocolate from the dispensing tray.

"Thank you," she said and smiled politely.

"Oh, by the way," said Ivor, "I'm glad I caught you. I've had a great thought on somewhere else you could visit. I tell you of all those attractions, far and wide, and forget about this on our very doorstep." He plucked a leaflet from the tourist stand and handed it over. "Nottingham Castle, it's just around the corner. I've remembered, there's an event on there today, nostalgia day or something like that. I just thought, if you had the energy, you'd enjoy it, get a sense of the history of the place and if you feel like a bit of culture there's a museum." Fang's body looked distracted, which had not gone unnoticed by Ivor who clenched his hands together in front of his chest. "Sorry, I'm bombarding you, still jet-lagged?"

"I guess."

"My advice would be, go to the castle get some fresh air, stay up as long as you can and drink plenty of fluids. Sorry, I must sound like your mother."

Fang's body returned a smile.

"I'll think about the castle, just around the corner you say?"

"That's right, a five-minute walk, well, ten minutes tops. There's a map on the back of the leaflet. They do nice cream teas in the café there, I'd recommend you try one."

Fang's body waved the chocolate bar in the air.

"Thanks for the help. Bye-bye." And with that, she turned and made for the stairs. Ivor looked on as a sympathetic smile spread across his face.

We followed Fang's body as she walked back up the staircase and along the first-floor corridor to her room. As her body opened the bedroom door, we dashed inside. I did not have time to think that this may have been an intrusion on my part but with the door now closed behind us then there was little point in worrying. The room had a distinctive feel and was not at all like the corporate style of so many of the hotel chains. A huge double bed, with an abundance of sumptuous pillows, stood on a thick patterned carpet and above the velvet headrest was a picture of an old sailing ship amid a stormy sea. At the front of the room was a stately looking desk, with its top inlaid with green leather, upon which was spread several more leaflets which Ivor must have handed over. Fang's body started eating the chocolate while studying the leaflet on Nottingham Castle. I could see Fang's curiosity mounting.

"Is it true that in the UK you love castles?" she asked.

"As a general rule, it is," I replied, as my mind started to meander. "Castles conjure up eerie thoughts of fairy tales, sorcerers and legends. They're also a sizeable reminder that the past was real. Castles give us a sense of history, even though much of the human detail has been lost."

"A history waiting to be re-discovered."

"That's right, we love looking back, you only have to look at the popularity of family trees here, trying to find lost ancestors from scraps of parish records and inscriptions on gravestones, not to mention our love of archaeology and antiques."

Fang's body had neatly placed the last piece of chocolate into her mouth and dropped the wrapper in the bin. She grabbed a hair tie and brush from her bag and stood in front of the long mirror by the side of the desk. Fang and I moved in line with the mirror and there we were, staring back at each other. It was immediately apparent that Fang's body could no more see our reflections than she could see us. She brushed through her golden-brown hair and then began to tie it up in a bun, taking great care to catch every strand and revealing her bare neck. Fang looked on with intent.

"I'm going to try an experiment," she said and gently placed the palm of her hand on her body's neck. As she did, her body wriggled, as if shaking dust from her shoulders. Fang took her hand away and looked back at me. "Did you see that?" I nodded. Fang put her hand back to her body's neck but this time with no effect. "I can feel resistance. You try." So, with Fang's body catching the last of the loose strands of hair, I hesitatingly placed my hand where Fang's had been. I too felt resistance but there was no reaction from her body. “The way my body shivered when I first touched her neck, what do you make of it?”

“Coincidence?”

“No, it was the exact moment.”

“You think she sensed you?”

“She sensed something, she shivered, maybe she felt a coldness and the second and third touches simply did not have the same effect. And if we can affect sensors then we must have some substance to us. Fascinating don’t you think?”

“Fang, doesn’t the presence of spirits bring on coldness, is that what happened?”

“Maybe, let’s keep experimenting. I’ve already discovered something.”

“What’s that?”

Fang pointed to several chocolate bar wrappers in the bin.

“She’s eating a lot more chocolate than I ever did.” Fang’s body put on her yellow coat, picked up her white cotton shoulder bag and dropped the castle leaflet in it. “Looks like we’re going out, to the Castle.”

“You’ll follow?”

“Yes. You must come along, see what else we can discover?”

“Of course,” I said without hesitation, pleased at the invite and, in truth, I’d hoped to spend the rest of the afternoon with my new friend. And so, we rushed to follow Fang’s body out of the hotel room, down the staircase and through the hotel doors. It was only once in the street that a small niggle at the back of my mind appeared; the way I had rushed to join Fang without question was uncharacteristic of me. Should I have been more cautious? I banished the thought, if Fang and I were spirits in some otherworld that ran parallel to the human one then it was better that we stuck together, no matter what the castle had in store for us.

CHAPTER FIVE

We soon found ourselves at the bottom of a huge outcrop of sandstone rock, its sheer face towering above us. As we looked up, over a hundred feet above our heads sat Nottingham Castle, perched at the very edge of the cliff top and looking imperiously across the city. Right beside us was an ancient inn with whitewashed walls and multi-pane windows bordered by black wooden frames. The rear of the inn was built into the rock, an indication of its antiquity, and I told Fang of how, in the twelfth century, Richard the Lionheart had allegedly set off for the crusades from this very place.

We followed the cobbled path that twisted around the cliff and then up towards the castle entrance. Tunnels in the sandstone rock appeared one after another, spilling out onto the neatly mown grass between the cliff face and the path. The entrances, carved into the rock, were sealed off with wrought iron railings making them look like so many medieval prison cells.

As we walked, I became aware that Fang kept swapping sides. First, she would be on my right then circle behind me to appear on my left, all the while asking questions. I gave answers as best I could as well as throwing in any incidental facts that came to mind. Occasionally, Fang would walk backwards just in front of me, and I took it as a sign of her eagerness to gauge my expression. Her mode of progression was most endearing, though I did not comment fearing that if I did then she may modify her ways, and I was happy with her fluttering around me.

We stopped at an interpretation panel, beside one of the tunnel entrances, which told of the fourteenth-century residents of the castle. Queen Isabella and Roger Mortimer, the first Earl of March, together murdered the Queen's husband, Edward II, so that they could seize regal powers. They were, however, brought to justice and now haunt the castle. She wanders the grounds in a white dress and he is trapped below in the cave where he had been held prisoner before his death. 'So, spirits can be trapped,' I thought with more than a little apprehension. The cave in question was the opening before us, named 'Mortimer's Hole' after the infamous Earl. I wondered if our strange state would give us the ability to see ghosts, and, though there was no sign of Mortimer behind the iron railings, I made a mental note to watch out for Isabella's white dress within the confines of the castle grounds.

Further along the path, a bronze statue of Robin Hood greened with age and posed to fire an arrow from his bow, guarded the entrance to the castle grounds. A cluster of people were gathered around the figure, eagerly awaiting turns for a photo with the legendary outlaw.

The entrance to the castle grounds was a long-arched tunnel which pierced the perimeter wall and stood between two broad turrets. A chalkboard announced 'Costume Day – see the past come to life.' Fang's body soon joined the gentle stream of visitors passing through the tunnel, which was cluttered with folk dressed in historical costume, mainly Victorian, some greeting visitors in their particular vernacular. There was even a teddy boy and girl, representing the 1950s, him sporting a bright red draped jacket and her a pale blue voluminous skirt. They certainly brought colour to the proceedings, and despite the dubious reputation of their subculture, several of the children, dressed as Victorian street urchins, ran excitedly around the pair. Fang's body smiled at the spectacle. The teddy boy and girl looked upwards with expressions of suppressed indignation, doing their best to ignore the fleeting interest of the children, who barely came up to the teddy girl's waistband. Fang's body stopped, dipped into her bag, retrieved her phone and took a photo of the scene before moving on.

As we were just about level with the enigmatic couple, one of the children span off at a tangent from the girl's dress and almost collided with us. Fang and I stopped in our tracks. The rest of the children followed excitedly and ran out from the half-light of the tunnel into the relative brightness of the castle grounds. The teddy boy looked at his partner and blew out his cheeks, I took this as his relief that their cool had been restored by the departure of the excitable entourage. In return, the teddy girl offered him a stick of chewing gum, which he gratefully accepted, and together they happily chewed away. We caught up with Fang's body who, unimpeded, now stood just inside the castle grounds, sipping at her bottle of water. A path followed the perimeter wall up to the castle around a hundred yards in front of us. The route was lined with several interpretation panels, the first of which I could just about read from the corner of my eye while appearing to look towards the castle.

"Would you like me to tell you some history of the castle?" I asked.

"Yes, of course," replied Fang eagerly.

"The castle was visited by Henry VIII in 1511, which was the last time a monarch stayed at the castle. In 1831 the original medieval castle was all but destroyed by fire during riots caused by the defeat of an electoral reform bill in Parliament. It wasn't until 1875 that the renovation began, turning the castle into a museum for fine art and resulting in the modern mansion building you see today."

"Wow, your knowledge is amazing," said Fang. I pointed to the panel from which I had cribbed my facts. Fang gave me a sideways glance. "Funny lah. Come on, we need to keep following my body, we don't want to lose her in the crowd."

The grass concourse was awash with people enjoying the autumn afternoon. Plenty had entered into the spirit of the occasion and dressed in costume, I was amazed at the number and the enthusiasm shown. The Victorian gentry and poor rubbed shoulders, as did soldiers and land girls from the 1940s. Even the outrageous fashion of the 1970s was represented. A pair of suffragettes, followed by the urchins from earlier, walked by clutching leaflets that they handed out to passers-by. Fang's body clicked away on her camera phone, capturing each successive spectacle.

In a cordoned-off area, towards the far perimeter wall was a group in medieval dress, a few with bows and quivers. A raised voice came from that direction, they were about to start an archery demonstration. Fang's body joined a clutch of spectators who were seated on a grass incline on the far side of the cordon, using a foldable shopping bag as an impromptu ground blanket. Fang and I took up position on either side of her.

As the demonstration started, a target was set around twenty yards from a cluster of archers. The crowd applauded at each successive bull's eye. As the demonstration wore on, I laid back and looked up to the heavens. It could have been a perfectly ordinary Saturday as I watched the cumulous clouds drift across the sky. Then the feeling that the clouds were stationary and it was I that was moving gently, perhaps on a sailing ship drifting eastward on a flat sea.

"Isn't it great, looking up at the clouds, watching them float by," I said, relaxing into the moment, "and each cloud seems to represent something. Look, there's a coyote's head."

"A coyote?" said Fang, lying back as I had done. "That's very specific, why a coyote?"

"Ah, well, a coyote has a distinctive long thin snout, longer than a fox or a wolf. Do you see it?"

"Not really, which one are you looking at,"

"Directly above, look." And I pointed.

"You know what? I just about see what you mean, and the cloud just behind it looks like a crocodile's mouth snapping at the coyote's head."

"I see it, and behind the crocodile is a rabbit. Do you

think it says something about me, seeing animals in clouds I mean?"

"That you have a vivid imagination."

"You're not wrong, I've been thinking all sorts since yesterday, I mean about being out-of-body." And my mind started to wander back to its dark, dangerous extremities. Fang turned to face me.

"Not a malignant force again?"

"No, something else."

"Tell me."

I made the mistake of talking off the top of my head, thoughts rolling out unfiltered and unchecked.

"I wonder if there is a reason for us being taken from our bodies. I mean, perhaps, I'm here for some sort of atonement, for something I've done. Who knows what dangers could be lurking right here in the castle? Perhaps, there's a conspiracy going on. Perhaps, everyone's in on it except me and you're luring me into a trap." As soon as I heard myself say the last sentence, I regretted it. I'd made a dreadful accusation; Fang had shown me only friendliness. Worse, when I thought back, then from the moment that we'd met, admittedly not long ago, I'd had faith in her. Why had I used those words? My meagre defence was that I was talking more in general than in particular and thoughts of Mortimer's Hole and the trapped spirit were fresh in my mind. Trouble was, I had said those words directly to Fang who was now looking back at me with a look of disenchantment, her smile gone, the bottom corners of her mouth turned down. It was the same look of upset that I'd observed in Lou when I had played the practical joke with the parking ticket. I'd shown a lack of empathy then and I'd shown another, with Fang, now. I felt despicable, and Fang had fallen uncharacteristically quiet. She sat up and then dipped her head, her eyes piercing me from beneath their brows. I sat up to face her.

"Fang, I didn't mean that last sentence." I couldn't even bear to repeat it. "It was just my wretched imagination running off." Fang said nothing. "I wasn't thinking."

"What's your imagination thinking now?"

"That you're never going to forgive me."

"Your imagination is right."

My heart sank, my friendship with Fang lying in ruins. It was now the corners of my mouth that turned down, a taste of my own thoughtless medicine.

"Fang, I'll never forgive myself for being such an idiot. I trust you completely, utterly."

"Hang on, I'd not finished my sentence. I was saying, your imagination is right, but only a fraction of the time. Sure, you're forgiven, I know you didn't mean it and it's nice to know you've faith in me."

I'd never felt such a relief, and I put my heightened emotion down to the infernal set of circumstances that we shared. Yet Fang was coping far better than I was. Often in a state of anxiety, and with a multitude of things going wrong, I found it hard to establish what was worrying me most. In the rarefied atmosphere of an out-of-body experience then it was hardly surprising that I had rambled incoherently. With equilibrium, and smiles, restored my thinking became clearer and I turned to my companion.

"Fang, can I share something with you?"

"Sure."

"Well, I guess what's bothering me is the way my

body is behaving. The problem is, what happens if he gets worse? I can't see him getting better. At the moment he is annoying but he could get violent. He could fall out with Lou. I can't deny that it's unsettling me." Fang drew in her lips, tight between her teeth, on my behalf, I thought, at first, but she could equally have been thinking of her own circumstances. "Fang, are you worried about the direction your body might take?"

She looked at her body who was scrolling intently on her phone.

"I've not got enough data. There are some differences I've noticed, but not enough to worry about, at the moment."

"How do you do it, remain so calm, I mean?"

"The thing is, Fred, how I put this?" Fang paused for a second, I gave an expectant smile, pleased she was considering my feelings. "You're such a worrier. Instead of seeing an opportunity, you see a problem." I thought for a moment, I'd heard similar words in the training courses that work had sent me on though, with no practical advice on how to make the required changes, I had returned to the office none the wiser. Fang prompted me. "Think about it, you're out of your body, what could you do?"

I thought earnestly, avoiding the peril of speaking off the top of my head. The parallel of Charles Dickens' Christmas Carol came to mind.

"If I followed my body, I would see how people interact with me."

"That's a stiff way of putting it."

"I guess, I was trying to say I'd find out who my friends are, though for that I'd have to follow them as well, sounds creepy."

"It's up to you, but that's what I would do. Think of Lou in particular, she seems to be the most important person to you."

I did not disagree.

"Thanks, Fang, that sounds like good advice."

"But we mustn't forget our other task, to find a way to rejoin our bodies, the clock's ticking. And, don't forget me either, understand?"

I nodded, in any case, how could I ever forget Fang?

CHAPTER SIX

A lengthy round of applause marked the end of the archery demonstration and the crowd started to disperse. The clouds above were gathering, their darkened undersides threatening rain, and Fang's body made towards the castle entrance at the top corner of the grounds. On the terrace outside, she stood square against the glass panelling that had replaced the stone wall at that part of the perimeter where even small children could enjoy the views without being lifted by adults. Beyond the glass was the sheer drop of the cliff face, and, far below our feet, the roof of the ancient inn jutted out from the rock.

Another notice board told us we were standing on the tip of a natural promontory known as the 'Castle Rock' and that we were one hundred and thirty feet above the ground. The view stretched from the city centre in the east to the leafy sprawl of the suburbs to the west. In the distance, to the south, and beyond the flood plain of the Trent, the low hills of Leicestershire gently mingled with the cloud cover.

Fang's body took another sip of water from her bottle and headed inside the castle entrance. After a short queue at the reception, she paid, holding her smartwatch against the card reader, and received the obligatory introduction speech; the foremost attraction was the long gallery and Fang's body wasted no time heading straight there.

The gallery was, as its name suggested, a long room with a high ceiling and clinically white walls which were crowded with paintings, I estimated over a hundred. It appeared that one side was given over to mainly landscapes while the other to mainly portraits. Fang's body looked up and down the gallery as if wondering where to start, before setting off down the wall of landscapes.

We followed Fang's body and stopped at each painting with her as she took time to appreciate the artwork. I felt quite at home, recognising several of the locations, and I added a little commentary as we went. It came to me that the paintings were arranged in a sort of timeline as the leafy green and precise Georgian landscapes gave way to nightmarish portrayals of the squalor which accompanied the industrial revolution. In one painting the decay of the early nineteenth-century slums was shown and in another, the misery bestowed upon workers as they left a mill. Both these paintings left me with a sense of distaste and I was glad as we moved on to the light relief provided by depictions of the city fair and modern Nottingham.

By the time we turned to walk down the opposite wall, the room had filled with a hubbub, some of the costumed participants of the day had made their way inside. The damp clothes of many of the newcomers told me that the rain had arrived. As we worked steadily back down the room admiring the historical portraits, Fang made an observation.

"Have you noticed that everyone in the portraits is painted with a downbeat expression?"

"That's the stiff upper lip of resilience, probably," I said, off the cuff, "I can imagine sitting for hours on end for a portrait, probably in a cold room, would do that to a face. Not many would have been painted in the height of summer."

Fang smiled. I realised that I had defaulted to the weather for an explanation, perhaps another trait of the British that Fang had heard of.

"Know what I think? If you had a portrait painted it would likely be for a moment of significance, an anniversary, for example. A portrait would have been quite an investment and, in those days, maybe the only time in a person's life their image would be captured. I can imagine that a Victorian would want to be remembered as a serious, respectable figure rather than risk coming across as silly or conceited, a smile can easily be interpreted as a smirk. See what I mean?"

Fang's logic seemed entirely plausible, and she had delivered her deduction with the sincerity of an analyst.

"I see exactly what you mean. I think you've hit the nail on the head, amazing." Fang pointed to a notice on the pedestal beside us, it was she who had surreptitiously cribbed the information this time. I groaned my realisation as Fang started a fit of giggles. "Funny lah," I offered then hesitated a moment, not quite understanding the meaning of what I had just said. "Did I get that right?"

Fang struggled to reply because she had burst into laughter but finally announced, "It was okay." She placed her palm flat across her chest as if relieved she had managed to get these few words out then the giggles set in again. Such was my pleasure in watching her reaction, my loneliness seemed a distant memory.

The next set of paintings, just beyond the alcove that divided the gallery, was a cluster of a dozen or so small portraits, all of the children. Although miniature in size, they were most lifelike and brightly coloured. Their expressions were neither a smile nor the serious stare that most of the portraits of adults had shown, perhaps, this was the style for children.

I was just wondering if these particular portraits were small because of their young subjects when a rhythmic click-clacking, which had been getting steadily louder, stopped. I turned around to see a casually dressed couple who had overtaken Fang's body and now stood looking back at the portrait section. The woman had a large brown leather, open-topped, shoulder bag and, with a pair of black heels, had undoubtedly been the source of the click-clacking. By her side was a man with collar-length hair swept back with gel and a salmon pink jumper draped over his shoulders.

"They're so small it was hardly worth the bother, eh?" he said, looking directly at the children's portraits.

"Huh, they wouldn't make the Tate, that's for sure, nothing in this gallery would," replied the woman.

"What do you expect from the provinces? I'd say the main attraction is the exit, wouldn't you?" The man snorted out a laugh, rejoicing in his sarcastic statement, and they both swiftly moved on.

Fang sensed my dismay, caused by their uncharitable

words.

"Ignore those two, and you know what?" she said. "These small portraits are my favourites."

"Me too," I concurred. "They have such curious expressions and look at the dimpled cheeks of the girl with the yellow dress and red hair, she looks like she's about to break into a smile. I wonder what the occasion could have been?" And I pointed to the smallest portrait of all. I drew nearer to examine the face more closely; was she smiling or not? I lost myself in the image before Fang prompted me, her body was now several paintings ahead of us and heading towards the exit of the room. We hurried to catch up. The room had left a fateful impression upon me, a feeling of a collection of people whose moments of significance had been captured, yet for many that significance had been lost and their painting stood hiding a mystery that could only be guessed at. A gallery of ghosts, ghouls and forgotten souls.

In the next few rooms, we found modern art and ceramics, all admirable but lacking the spirit that the paintings in the long gallery had generated. This disconnection with the exhibits continued until we entered a small room that was filled with a collection of curiosities and labelled 'Objects of Emotion.' Fang's body stopped at a glass display cabinet with only three items. They looked old but commonplace: an antique pocket watch, a ceramic bowl and a doll. The notice below the label described how objects have the power to evoke strong emotions, I baulked at the concept. Nevertheless, I read on. An example given was a gift from a person who has since died will stay with you as a memento and a bond with the past; the loss of such an object would cause intense sorrow, far beyond monetary value. I started to realise what the display was trying to say. The notice invited visitors to suppose the significance of each of the objects. Fang and I were up for the challenge.

I found myself focused on the watch. The silver-coloured case looked dull and leaden, small scuffs marked it out as well used. Had the watch been a cherished retirement gift and given as a piece of jewellery? I shared my thoughts with Fang who had other ideas.

"There's a lot of wear for a cherished retirement gift. I think it is more likely it's had a lifetime's use. It's large enough, so surely a gentleman's watch. It has a plain case and dial so I think this would rule out the piece as jewellery. Besides, a piece of jewellery would be looked after so why the accumulated damage? Maybe, it was used by someone who needed to constantly refer to it, who needed to know the precise time. Maybe, a person whose work brought them into contact with a timetable, someone who worked on a railway, a guard and it was part of their equipment supplied by their employer, like a whistle or a torch. What do you think?"

I was hugely impressed by Fang's deduction, her logic felt infallible. I looked around for an explanatory notice but there wasn't one. Fang's deduction was her own.

"Fang, that all fits together, you're much better at this than I am."

As the Display cabinet was glass on all sides, I manoeuvred to the rear panel so that I could see the face of the watch case which was flipped up. I stood in amazement when I saw the letters MR engraved on the case and underneath the number 309. My time waiting for trains at Nottingham station had not been wasted for

I had read the board on the history of the local railways many times and I knew exactly what MR stood for.

"Fang, you have a talent, the letters MR are marked on the watch case, that is the 'Midlands Railway,' I'm sure of it. The number probably indicates this was the three hundred and ninth watch made for the company. But why would it cause emotion?"

"Maybe, the employee was allowed to keep the watch after retirement, maybe it was a retirement gift, of sorts, after all." I puffed up my chest, it seemed my guess had not been totally adrift. "After years of dedication to duty, the object would have been much coveted, it would have been natural that his loved ones would see the watch as almost the essence of that person."

I looked around, what had seemed to be a room of dull, faded antiquities now seemed to be bursting with life, each object wanting to tell their stories and that of their human custodians. I felt a tinge of regret, before I moved into Lou's I had developed a habit of travelling light and, consequently, had collected few meaningful possessions. The closest thing I owned to an object of emotion was my phone, more due to the sports results it delivered than any sentimental value. Our tour of the castle had affected me greatly, at least the older objects within it had. I felt an empathy with history and an understanding of just how close the past is to us should we care to reach for it. I was developing a spiritual side and the idea that Fang and I were truly spirits strengthened its grip.

CHAPTER SEVEN

The small room of objects led out into a gift shop, which housed the usual array of toy weapons, pewter trinkets and assorted stationery. Beyond was a café and between the two rooms was the obligatory information board, with details of local attractions. Fang's body briefly studied the board before moving to the café counter where she ordered a cream tea. The café was a long narrow room with a row of full-height bay windows which overlooked the cliff-top terrace outside.

Fang's body took an empty table beside one of the bay windows and looked out onto the view that we had much admired earlier. Fang and I squeezed into spare chairs on either side of her body and watched the comings and goings. As the cafe thinned, a youthful-looking waiter approached and began clearing the adjacent table. Fang's body topped her tea up with the last drops from the teapot as the waiter watched on. As soon as Fang's body caught his eye, he took the opportunity to start a conversation.

"Hi, is this your first visit to the castle?" he asked, flicking his long fringe back with a quick turn of his head.

"Yes, I'm from Singapore," replied Fang's body with a faint smile. "I'm here for two weeks on business."

"Really, well welcome, what do you think of it?"

"The view from here is amazing, it stretches out so far." The waiter followed Fang's body's gaze to the vista across the terrace.

"Those hills in the distance are in rural Leicestershire, I reckon you can see thirty or forty miles south from here." Fang's body turned back to the waiter, her eyes appeared quite different to Fang's, darker, more concentrated. I looked over to Fang to see that she was staring intently at her body, seemingly studying what changes in manner had occurred since the strike. The waiter continued. "Do you get cream teas in Singapore?"

"Oh yes, not that I have them often. I heard they are a speciality here so had to try one." It was noticeable, to me at least, that in contrast to Fang, her body was not asking questions directly, however, this did not seem to stop the waiter's enthusiasm in supplying information.

"Do you know, we drink more tea than water, beer or anything else? We are, in fact, the only country in the world where tea is the most popular drink, water is top of the list in every other country so you could say that we're unique."

"That's an amazing fact."

"Thank you. I surprise myself sometimes with what I know. I pick up lots of facts working here, with all the conversations that take place then it's kind of subliminal. I hear all sorts, like there's not a single point in Britain more than eighty-four miles from the coast, the town furthest from the sea is Lichfield, not too far from here.

And here's another one for you, the UK's national dish is chicken tikka masala."

"Not fish and chips?"

"Nope, amazing isn't it? Chicken tikka is an Indian dish, the masala was added because the British love a sauce with their meat, think of roast beef and gravy." Fang's body looked as amazed as I did, the shift in national cuisine had passed me by, though admittedly masala was one of my favourites. "Hey, tell me some facts about Singapore?"

"Sure. We are not just one main island; Singapore comprises of sixty-three different islands. We are a city-state, like the Vatican, and sometimes referred to as the garden island. We are modern, clean and environmentally friendly. The centre point of mainland Singapore is MacRitchie Reservoir, probably no more than ten miles from the sea. Oh, our national dish is chicken too, chicken rice."

"I feel I know the place. Chicken rice? I'll look the recipe up and try it."

"If you do, use ginger root and serve it with chilli sauce."

"I will. Hey, if you want a memento of your visit, I know just the place?"

"The castle gift shop?"

"Oh no, that's for school kids. This place is in the city, just outside the indoor shopping centre. They sell all sorts of things in the way of souvenirs: bits of jewellery, authentic Nottingham lace, old books, that sort of stuff. It's kind of an antiques shop and I've heard it mentioned quite a few times in here, you'll get a little bit of history there. I'll write the address down if you like?"

"For sure."

And he started to scribble details on his order pad. I looked over his shoulder to see 'All Things Past and Present, Canal Street' emerge on the paper and then a sketched map.

"If you go, mention you heard about them from the Castle Cafe." He placed the slip of paper on the table in front of Fang's body and looked across at the clock. "I must get on, it was nice talking to you, come back if you can and thanks for the information, I'll be sure to pass it on, MacRitchie Reservoir, wasn't it? Oh good." And with that, he disappeared into the kitchen. I looked over at Fang, blowing my cheeks out, still wondering about chicken tikka masala.

"Seems like a nice chap?" I commented.

"He was keen to tell my body about this shop," replied Fang.

"What makes you think that?"

"As soon as he passed the information, he made an excuse and left."

"But he had things to do."

"That's what he said but it's not very busy in here, most of the tables have been cleared. And, he went to the trouble of drawing a map."

Having looked around, most of the tables were indeed empty but in the far end of the café were the pompous couple from the gallery. He was having a conversation on his phone, aided by a bright red set of earbuds, and she was tapping away on a tablet. As I watched, the woman stood up, uttered a few words, placed the tablet in her shoulder bag, which she left on the chair, and made off in the direction of the toilets.

"You're still upset," said Fang, noticing my direction of gaze and, no doubt, my stern expression.

"I don't like snobbery that's all," I replied. "Was I scouring?"

"Yes. Come with me. I have an idea." We were soon standing over the lady's chair, the tablet staring brightly up at us from the dark recess of the abandoned shoulder bag. "If we can affect sensors then we should be able to use touch screens, follow my finger with yours." Fang's assertion was correct, and within a few dabs, we had a folder of apps open. My heart jumped; our earthly ability to use touch screens opened up a host of possibilities but for now, Fang was focused on the job in hand. "She has many social media accounts. We could send a message saying how the castle gallery is a must-see."

"Oh, that might be going too far."

"Okay, let's set the alarm to go off." I smiled at the thought of Fang's new suggestion. "To go off at 3 am." My smile widened. "I'll change the alarm sound to a scream."

I coughed out a laugh, the idea was irresistible.

"Let's do it."

Fang's finger darted back and forth from settings to the clock then the internet. It was all I could do to keep up but could see that a creepy yell from the web had been chosen for the alarm sound.

"All done," announced Fang.

We returned to the table to see that Fang's body had drunk the remaining tea. She stood up to leave, yawning behind a raised hand as she did. It was a little past four o'clock. Fang reminded me of the time difference; it would be eleven o'clock at night in Singapore and it was likely that her body would return to the hotel to sleep. We followed Fang's body out of the castle grounds and back down the wet cobbles, a drizzly rain still falling. This time there was no one around the Robin Hood statue. Fang's body took her phone from her bag and started lining up one more photo. Fang jumped in front of the statue and replicated the pose of the famous outlaw before turning in my direction.

"Come on, do the pose with me."

"We might be seen by the camera," I replied, thinking of stories of old black and white photographs where shadowy apparitions hover in the background.

"I doubt it, if we do appear then I expect my body will jump from her skin with shock, you would then have three of us to contend with."

I did not say anything, just smiled. I would not have minded three Fang's and there had been nothing to contend with, on the contrary, it had been an enchanting afternoon in the company of Fang and her body and my misgivings about rushing to the castle had been dispelled. With photos taken, and no apparitions appearing in the camera, we continued our descent and retraced our steps back through the city streets. As we approached the hotel doors, my mind turned back to domestic matters.

"Should we meet up tomorrow morning back in the lobby to compare notes? I mean, I ought to go back to the hospital now, see how my body is getting on."

"Perfect, if we try between ten and eleven o'clock." I understood there could be many complications that could foil the timing but was relieved that we had agreed to meet again. Fang rushed to the door to slip through beside her body, waved goodbye and was gone.

I turned and headed back to the hospital, the icy tendrils of loneliness already beginning their work. I felt a little lost without my companion fluttering around me.

At the start of the day, I thought that I would be her guide and take her under my wing, now it felt the other way round. I thought of her charming ways, her laugh, her smile, her unusual intelligence, her enthusiasm and her undeniable curiosity. With Fang, my ordeal had turned to adventure and as much as I wanted to rejoin my body, and restore the natural order, I was now hoping that my excursion out of humanity would last a little longer. Tomorrow and my rendezvous with Fang could not come soon enough.

CHAPTER EIGHT

The new morning at the hospital was heralded by the eight o'clock routine checks, and I had woken to see my body with a thermometer hanging from his lips once more. The previous evening had been spent observing my body, not that there was much to observe as, with earbuds in, he had paid little attention to anything other than his phone.

Lou must have paid a visit judging from the half-empty packet of gingernut biscuits and selection of phone accessories scattered across the overbed table. She had also brought a handmade get well soon card, the message inside read, 'You would do anything to get out of the gardening.' I was reminded that we were going to spend some of the weekend tidying up the back garden together, and I had been looking forward to it.

As the evening had drawn on and the skies outside darkened, so had my mood. My mind started to find new things to worry about. Were there others in this state of limbo that were remaining hidden for some malignant purpose? If Fang and I could affect sensors then could sensors detect us and were we been tracked somehow? What about my body, would his poor behaviour deteriorate further, would he be capable of criminal acts? And, worst of all, was my friendship with Lou about to be destroyed. If I did not reunite with my body soon, what would I be getting back into? Amidst these thoughts, I had fallen asleep, only to wake beside my disgruntled, ungrateful self once again.

"I'm being discharged today, why are you bothering with my readings?" said my body as the nurse retrieved the thermometer from his lips. I cringed.

"It's the ward procedure," said the nurse, "and I wouldn't be too sure about being discharged until the doctor's rounds, they can soon change their minds you know, if your temperature was very high."

"It isn't, is it?"

"No, I'm just saying, wait and see what the doctors say."

I sat impatiently. I was anxious to meet up with Fang but equally so to hear what the doctor would say about my body's health, so I decided to hang around for a while. It was just after ten o'clock when my thoughts were interrupted by the doctor's entourage swiftly assembling around the bed.

"Your tests have all come back clear, how do you feel?" said the doctor who appeared to be the most senior among the group.

"I feel fine, I just want to get home."

"That's good to hear, you've been lucky by the sound of things, a lightning strike can be deadly. As soon as the discharge paperwork is done you can go."

"And when will that be?"

"Before lunchtime, it depends on how busy they are up here."

My body did not look too pleased at the timescale and puffed his cheeks out. Having no appetite to hear what else he had to say and eager to meet up with Fang, I left.

It was around quarter to eleven when I reached the hotel and, to my relief, found Fang sitting in one of the comfy chairs. She waved me over and from her expression of suppressed excitement it looked like she had something of importance to say. I took the chair beside her.

"Look, over there," she said and nodded towards the reception desk. "The laptop that the receptionists use for booking in guests, the one on the desk just under the counter, has a touch screen. The receptionist who's on duty often goes into the back office for long periods, when the lobby is empty, which leaves the laptop free and out of their sight. Ivor's not in this morning, it's a new guy. Next time he leaves we should try to make the touchscreen work, get on the internet and find out about out-of-body experiences, there's some crazy stuff on there and we might find some answers."

"Sounds good. Oh, by the way, I have some news; my body will be discharged today, perhaps even this morning."

"That's great."

"Hmm." I sat back in contemplation.

As we waited for the lobby to empty, a clutch of guests, who had been gathering by the reception, started to leave the hotel together. I had been watching closely to see if any of them would make eye contact, still convinced that there may be spirits at large. When one of their number walked over to us, only to pick up a menu from the table in front, I momentarily thought he had seen us, it stirred me. My worries from the night before flooded back. After the guests had left, I turned to Fang.

"Do you think there are other spirits out there who can see us but for some reason are not revealing themselves?"

"Why wouldn't they reveal themselves?" replied Fang.

"I'm not sure. Perhaps, they're following us for some purpose."

"Mm, we should at least keep vigilant, I'm sure my body is going shopping today, at least she's been browsing city centre shops on her phone. She's had breakfast and gone up to her room. When she leaves, we should follow and see if we can find any other spirits around the city."

I agreed and was about to share another of my worries but hesitated, perhaps it would be better if I just let the day unfold without continually rolling out my fears.

"You were going to say something?" asked Fang.

"It was nothing."

"You're worried about Lou, more than ever?"

I stared at my friend in amazement.

"Fang, I swear you have magical powers. How did you know I was thinking that?"

Fang purred at the compliment.

"It's not so difficult."

"How though?"

"When you told me your body was to be discharged, you did not look too pleased about it. Naturally, he would probably go home to Lou and you mentioned your fears in that direction yesterday, you were worrying about how your body may behave with her. Also, having already spoken about one of your fears, why not mention another? You looked as if you were going to speak then stopped, why? If the reason was shyness, the fear could involve a personal affair, and I thought of Lou again. With Lou appearing twice in my reasoning, surely it was a worry about Lou you were wanting to mention. Simple."

I shook my head; the logic was clear enough but I found Fang's powers of reasoning far from simple.

"Remarkable Fang, you summed things up nicely. I'll be a lot happier when we find a way to get back inside our bodies."

"Here's a plan, we'll follow my body, when she appears, and keep a lookout for other spirits. We should be okay if we stick together but, at some point, you should go back home to observe your body and Lou like we spoke about. We can meet up here again tomorrow." Fang suddenly sat upright. "Look, there is no one at reception now. We should try to work the touch screen and see what the internet has to say?"

We climbed over the counter and stood in front of the laptop. We put our fingers together and touched the screen and up came the password cue.

"It is L, zero, b, b, Y, $," said Fang. "I've been watching. Let's see if we can use the keyboard, follow my finger." We found that we could not, the mechanical nature of the keys had offered just too much resistance. "That was just a long shot, let's try the touch screen, follow my finger." I did as Fang asked and in quick succession, the screen keyboard popped up, the password was entered and the desktop with all its icons appeared. We excitedly discussed sending our bodies an email but quickly agreed that any attempt at communication would need careful contemplation. How would our bodies react if they received an email purporting to be from their invisible double? In any case, it was hard to figure out how our bodies could help and searching the internet seemed to offer a better hope of finding answers.

Any suggestions on what we should search for?" asked Fang.

"Out-of-body how to get back in," I replied with the utmost seriousness.

We set off on our internet search with my finger following Fang's across the screen. A deluge of information came up and we rapidly searched for articles of relevance. My expectations of finding anything useful were not that high and after a couple of minutes of surfing, they were lower. The articles spoke about floating sensations or a feeling of looking down from above while the physical body lay motionless. Among many others, causes of out-of-body experiences were put down to brain irregularities, drug use and sleep disorders. None talked about how to get back into a body, this seemed to happen automatically after the experience was over with no deliberate act on the part of the sufferer. As link lead to link, we got distracted by an article that described a phenomenon called cerebral meandering, the ability of the brain to think through problems while the person is occupied with other things. When driving a car, for example, a solution to a long-standing problem can be thrown out into the conscious mind in a eureka moment. The article got even more fascinating. We learnt about the nervous system in our bodies and that electricity is required to send signals throughout the body and to the brain, making it possible for us to move, think and feel. The most impressive fact of all was that the energy required in processing thoughts was around twenty-five watts, enough to power a light bulb.

"Let's try just 'out-of-body experience,'" Fang said, hoping this would refocus our search.

We scrolled through the new set of articles that had duly appeared, some referred to academic journals, some to courses but it was an event that caught my attention, one which was close to home. I alerted Fang and we soon had details on the screen.

"A seminar on neuroscience," I said, "and there's a lecture on out-of-body experiences by someone from the British Guild of Metaphysicians. It's on Tuesday afternoon and even better it's at Loughborough, which isn't that far away from here?"

"We should go," said Fang with widened eyes that told me she was seeing possibilities.

"Definitely, I've been thinking of going back to college, here's my chance to have a taster. We can get the train from Nottingham; it should only take half an hour to get there."

We both absorbed the details to find the venue was a hall within a local college and within walking distance from the railway station. With no other article measuring up to the fervour caused by the seminar, we tried another search, this time on 'lightning strikes out-of-body.'

The first article that came up looked promising, we clicked on the link and were immediately hooked. A description was given of a man who had been struck by lightning at a family barbeque and found himself thrown backwards into the air. The drama occurred on a humid, overcast afternoon though the strike was unexpected as there had been no rain. The man had picked himself up only to realise that the body before him, lying prostrate on the ground, was his own. As his family rushed to his body, the man realised that he was invisible to others. The man's story matched what Fang and I had both experienced. I looked up to check Fang's expression to see she was staring into the hotel lobby. I followed her gaze and there was Fang's body walking towards the hotel exit.

"Quick, we need to follow," said Fang, "we can resume our search later." We both scuttled over the counter and just caught Fang's body as she walked through the hotel doors. Once in the street, Fang's body marched along at double pace, swerving skilfully past oncoming pedestrians, Fang explained that Singapore has the highest speed of pedestrian walkers in the world, helped by a one-way system in busy streets.

I lost count of how many shops we went in, some in department stores, some in shopping centres, some which lined the main pedestrian ways and some tucked away in back streets. It was early afternoon by the time we took a break and Fang's body stopped off at a bakery in the indoor shopping centre to buy a traditional Cornish pasty. After finding a bench seat, which backed onto a water fountain, in the central hall, she started her lunch.

Fang and I had a chance to compare notes in relative calm though neither of us had seen the slightest indication of a spirit. There had been no one who stood out from the commonplace, no one who had made eye contact and no one who had sensed us. I joked that our next internet search should be 'how to find spirits.' We vowed to keep vigilant.

Fang's body rose to her feet and made her way to the shopping centre exit. Just outside was a beleaguered shop front sign that announced 'All Things Past and Present,' the place the waiter from the castle had recommended. Inside was packed with tables, cabinets and dressers all crammed with plates, jugs, books, figurines and every type of trinket imaginable. A yellow strip had been painted onto the floor to help customers navigate the muddled thoroughfare created by the assortment of old furniture, urns and stacks of books. Fang's body ventured further into the shop passing chimney pots full of walking sticks and chairs stacked with board games. She must have wondered what she had walked into, and I could not have imagined a more ramshackle collection of objects. Still, the strange place attracted customers with several manoeuvring in the depths of the shop, which stretched out so far among the clutter that it was difficult to make out where the shop ended. As Fang and I stared in that direction, a voice sounded from behind us.

"Can I help?" We turned to see a white-haired lady, with kind eyes and henna-style tattoos protruding from her white cotton sleeves. She seemed to have appeared from a doorway in the side wall and Fang's body had jumped a little in surprise before turning around to face the lady.

"Hi, I hope you can. I'm looking for a memento," said Fang's body. "I'm visiting from Singapore and hoping to find something to remind me of my visit."

"A memento?"

"Yes, oh, the waiter from the castle café recommended you."

"The waiter? You know he keeps doing that, I have no idea why, but still, it keeps nice customers coming in so I shouldn't grumble. Have you any idea what sort of thing you'd like? An old book perhaps, we have plenty on Nottingham."

"I was thinking more about something I could wear, something old, something small, something like a charm."

"I have an idea, wait here." The shopkeeper made her way towards the back of the shambolic room. As she threaded through the cramped gangway, a couple drew aside to let her pass, gently nodding their acknowledgement before returning to their meanderings. Her destination was a large oak dresser which was laden with jewellery behind diamond leaded glass. After finding the right key, she returned with a tray of pendants. "These all originate from the local area, how about this one?" And she handed Fang's body a pendant with a lion's head motif. Fang's body held the dainty object in her hand to examine its details. With the high relief of its wavy mane, the lustre of gold and red cabochon eyes it was as intricate as it was dainty. "You'll hardly know you have it on it's such a light piece, designed for a lady, and made from a type of brass called pinchbeck, a mixture of copper and zinc formulated to look like gold but less dense. The alloy was popular in the early nineteenth century."

"It's so delicate."

"You can have it for ten pounds. Do you like it?"

"I love it, and thank you, I'll have it. I'll wear it now if I may."

"Of course." And with that, the shopkeeper fiddled with the clasp on the chain and placed the pendant around Fang's body's neck, the motif dropping just below the neckline of her top. My gaze finally left the lion's head and I turned to Fang.

"That's odd, of all the pendants on the tray, that's the one I would have picked too."

"You know the lion's head is the symbol of Singapore?" replied Fang. "It symbolises courage and inspires us to be brave."

"I think I did know that."

"Then maybe that's what drew you to the pendant, with me being by your side, perhaps the shopkeeper is thinking along the same lines too. The pendant connects Nottingham to Singapore, it's the perfect memento."

Fang's explanation seemed reasonable enough, then again, the trinket was eye-catching in its own right, to me at least. Fang's body paid the shopkeeper, who she thanked profusely, and left the shop. Outside, quite a crowd had gathered, and I wondered if the waiter had had great success in diverting his customers to this long shop of curiosities. However, as we got clear of the crowd and looked back the real reason became apparent; the shop was adjacent to the entrance to the City Caves, a popular tourist attraction and the disorderly queue for the afternoon tour had simply snaked around the shop front.

Fang's body headed back in the direction of the hotel; the shopping trip was over. With Fang's body back in her room, we sat in our usual comfy chairs waiting for an opportunity to use the reception laptop. We were in luck; it was not long before the lobby emptied and the receptionist left the front desk for the backroom. We climbed over the counter, checked the receptionist was safely occupied and stood facing the laptop.

We quickly re-found the article on the man struck by lightning at a barbeque and read on in fascination as it described how the man had assumed his body was dying so left the scene and started to ascend the stairs in his house to find his daughter. At this point, his account began to depart from our experience. His body began to transform from his own image and by the time he reached the top of the stairs, he was a ball of energy and thought, a spirit ready to move on to the beyond. He described how he could still move at will and went to his daughter's bedroom where he saw her reading. He felt totally at peace, despite the awful circumstances, and found himself on the edge of another dimension when, without warning, he was back in his body feeling pain. He had been revived by a neighbour carrying out CPR.

The most compelling part of the account was the man felt sure his consciousness had been released and the experience was not a hallucination. He was later able to describe the book his daughter was reading, a fact he could not have known. Fang and I were both riveted. Our spirits had been released yet we had not transitioned to a ball of thought which seemed to herald the passage to the beyond. Without warning, a hand came between ours, it was the receptionist. We both jumped back in shock, giving us no time to close the browser window.

The receptionist looked spooked, seeing the contents of the screen he must have surmised someone had interfered with the laptop, but how? There were no guests in the lobby and no other staff around. The content of the article could hardly have been spookier;

would his mind have the audacity to suspect a spirit presence? As he continued to muse, we returned to our seats and I found myself unsettled by the disturbance.

"We should be more careful," I said. "They might send for an exorcist and then who knows what would happen?"

Fang looked at me as if a little surprised.

"How would words and a sprinkle of holy water affect us?"

"It's just isn't that how a spirit presence is moved on, an exorcism?"

"I don't think we need worry about rituals and, in any case, he'll search for a more plausible explanation before ever settling on a spirit presence. I still think we're spirits though, but there's a difference between us and the man in the article, he died as a result of the strike and shortly after was resuscitated. It was death that released his spirit and resuscitation that brought it back. We did not die. I'm thinking that the lightning prompted some mechanism, some fake death rattle, that fooled our spirits into leaving our bodies, but there was no resuscitation, no signal, to pull our spirits back. What if we are now free spirits held back on the earth? As I said, we did not die, how can we pass over to the beyond, whatever the beyond is?"

"We're being held back by our living bodies."

"That's what I think and that is a huge problem for us. After all, we can hardly wait around for our bodies to die and then to be resuscitated before we can re-join them."

"I see." And I did see, what Fang had said made sense and the gravity of the situation was dawning on me, there might be no return. I made light of the situation with an observation. "Mind you, it won't be long before I do die from the number of gingernuts my body is eating, all that sugar can't be good for the heart." Fang tightened her lips as she considered my remark. "Fang, I'm more worried now than ever, how are we going to get back?" Her expression lightened.

"The pathway back could be for our bodies to experience something like a lightning strike, perhaps whatever it was that signalled our fake death could equally signal a fake recovery. Maybe, one of the effects of lightning, the noise, the heat, the magnetic field, who knows?"

Fang remembered from her schooldays that although lightning was commonplace, its nature is not easily explained. She described how lightning was a major inconvenience in Singapore and, while many mitigations were in place to avoid personal injury and structural damage, lightning acted in a seemingly random fashion, unimpressed by human theories and as if Zeus himself decided where strikes fell. As I sat back in contemplation, and with time pressing, it was not long before I thought of Lou. I turned to Fang.

"I ought to go back home now, see how my body is behaving. I should also follow him to work tomorrow, if he goes in that is, watch what happens. Things could get messy with my body's attitude. I can tell you all about it tomorrow if we meet here for about six."

"Sure, and we can compare experiences," replied Fang. "It's my first day in the Nottingham office and who knows how that will go. I'm glad we can share our news."

"So am I." And I truly was for who knew how our earthly lives could fall apart in the next twenty-four hours.

CHAPTER NINE

Lou's house was a two-bedroomed terrace at the end of a cul-de-sac. I arrived to see her car on charge and parked snugly on the drive that ran along the gable. The clicks and creaks of the cooling motor made me wonder if Lou and my body had only recently returned from the hospital. Despite the fading light, the front room curtains were still open, inside was unlit and unoccupied. One of Lou's scripts for a school play rested on the low coffee table and her favourite knitted cardigan was draped over the arm of the settee, I remembered she spoke about darning the elbows and had struggled to get wool of the same mustard shade.

School plays were not Lou's only passion, she worried much about the environment and had adopted a make do and mend philosophy with clothes. Nevertheless, she always appeared stylish, particularly in comparison to me, and her clothes seemed timeless. When special occasions demanded it, she would rent suitable attire from the internet, not wanting to buy something she was likely to wear only a few times.

I started to move to the back of the house, perhaps, my body and Lou were having dinner in the kitchen. Lou and I had grown into the habit of eating together and, as a consequence, my diet had improved considerably. Gone was the fast and easy food of my younger days, pizzas, pies and takeaways. Lou loved homemade bread, homemade soup and had a repertoire of dishes from around the world. My meagre offering in the department of international cuisine was, until recently, a Spanish omelette. Lou had the idea of increasing my range by teaching me a few simple dishes and we started with chilli con carne. Such was Lou's desire to eat well that the fruit bowl was constantly refilled and such was her hatred of waste that if any bananas looked like going over then they were made into banana bread, and if any bread had gone stale then it was repurposed into bread-and-butter pudding.

As I reached the rear wall, I was pulled from my thoughts by a raised voice from within the house and, although muffled by the masonry, there was no mistaking the tone, it was mine. I rushed to the kitchen window and peered in through the bottom of the blind, a flash of metal caught my eye. My body was by the worktop and facing me with a pinpoint stare, a bread knife gripped in his tightened fist. Behind him was Lou, looking upset. My body turned quickly towards her and waved the knife, I heard his raised voice again but still could not quite make out the words.

I looked on in horror, Lou and I always got along, the only time voices were raised was in the high jinks of our practical jokes. What I saw in front of me did not look like a practical joke. Was he really, threatening her with a knife? I banged my fist on the window, of course to no effect. The scene unfolded with me as a spectator, no more able to help than the leaves rustling in the breeze behind me on the patio. Then my body turned back to the worktop where a homemade loaf of bread sat on the cutting board with several slices cut from it. To my immense relief, there was at least a reason he had a bread knife, even if he had waved it. Lou shook her head and walked out into the hall. My relief was not complete though, why the heated exchange? Then another thought, Lou had likely made a fresh loaf specifically to welcome my body home and to the sin of aggressiveness he had added ingratitude. It felt like the horror of a nightmare was unfolding in front of me. I would have to watch as my body dismantled my life.

He moved to the kitchen table and sat with his back to me, hunched over, eating a sandwich made from two chunks of bread. The kitchen clock showed just after ten past six. With nothing remarkable happening, I moved back around to the front window. Lou had switched the light on and had nestled into the settee, busy darning the elbow of her cardigan. She was working impatiently, a sure sign she was upset. Her expression was one of concentration, her lips moving ever so slightly as if whispering to herself. I'd not seen her do this before, was this a sign of indignation? I stood and watched for the sake of watching. In truth, I couldn't take my eyes off her. I remembered evenings that we had spent together in that very room sharing stories, binge-watching cosy detective dramas and practising lines from her school plays. Having finished darning, she held her handy work up to the light for inspection. Seemingly satisfied, she draped the cardigan back over the arm of the settee.

Then a surprise, she was looking directly at me, her face changed again as her eyes narrowed. Had she sensed me peering in? She stood, walked to the window and drew the curtains.

Of course, she couldn't have sensed me, no one but Fang had for a full two days, perhaps no one else ever would. I walked to the back of the house again, my body had shut the blind. I sat on the bench under the window from where I might be able to hear voices but, probably, only if they were raised and this was the last thing I wanted.

My earthly future was heading in exactly the direction that I had feared courtesy of my body's shortcomings. If I felt love and concern, was he left with the balance of hate and disregard? I stayed put, hoping the back door might be opened for some reason so I could get in and watch how the evening developed inside. As the first stars appeared in the night sky my mind wandered to work. There was every chance that my body might not go in. There had been many Monday mornings when I had thought about taking a sickie though Lou's presence was always enough to chivvy me along. The reason for my reluctance centred around my new role in business management. The work involved ensuring that startup businesses were given the best chance of success by ensuring they received all the grants they were entitled to. This meant a lot of paperwork which included balance sheet projections, local impact statements and business risk assessments. The role also involved a lot of responsibility; the statements and figures used in any document had to be grounded and accurate. Any misrepresentations, apart from being unethical, could cause reputational damage and the transgressors disciplined by law. Lately, the management interpretation of grounded and accurate was becoming loose, and I had begun to lose sleep over it. They had started to encourage optimistic business projections to secure the success of grant applications. In practice, the businesses were hugely overvalued and their chances of success overrated. Not that they wouldn't tick along for a few years, what with a bank balance brimming with grants, but if a downturn came then they would not have the resilience to survive.

But the overwhelming reason for my Monday morning reticence was the weekly review meeting at nine o'clock where the progress of applications was reviewed with vigour. Anyone whose project was falling short of expectations was put under duress to sharpen matters up, and my project was falling short.

CHAPTER TEN

I had barely awakened from my night on the bench when I heard the kitchen roller blind spring open behind me. There was Lou, sporting the cardigan she had darned the night before and ready to face the pandemonium that seemed to be the norm at her school. Not that Lou minded, she took it all in her stride and, in the evening, usually gave me an amusing slant on the events that had unfolded during the day. And I never tired of listening to her accounts.

As Lou ate her cereal, I noticed she had made two cups of tea, a sign that my body was at least getting up and, sure enough, he appeared wearing my usual work attire. I always wore black trousers and a navy shirt at the office, it took the decision-making out of choosing what to wear. Lou and my body were not saying much, the mood appeared indifferent. At quarter past eight, they left the house. Lou unplugged the car, clicked the doors open and my body got in. I now saw exactly the problem Fang must have had at the station car park. I had harboured an idea that I would manoeuvre myself past my body when he opened the car door, but such was his speed that I did not get the chance. As Lou opened the boot to deposit her school bag, another idea occurred to me and I jumped in, dropping to the floor as the hatchback lid came down. As we set off, I found the sense of claustrophobia played on my nerves; what would happen if we were in an accident? I could be trapped for hours, days even. My imagination was running wild again and I vowed that next time I would skip the lift and get the tram.

The journey itself was uneventful with the road noise and radio masking any conversation between Lou and my body; I imagined a strained silence. After arriving at the school car park, they exchanged curt goodbyes and Lou opened the boot allowing me to make my escape. I joined my body and within five minutes we were outside my office block.

The company had given us a degree of flexibility in that employees could start anytime between eight and nine o'clock, and my lift with Lou delivered me to the office at a comfortable quarter to nine. It was a modern five-storey building with a large ground-floor reception area, which had a set of stairs leading to all floors. There was a mix of organisations that used the office block, though ours was the largest and had exclusive access to the second and third floors. My desk was on the second floor, with most of my colleagues, in an open-plan office with conference rooms at both ends and a small kitchen towards the centre. Air-conditioned and rich in natural light, it was a pleasant enough space to work in and, with the tram stop next to the building, the city centre amenities were only a short ride away.

I sat at an island of four desks in the business section with two colleagues, Rachel and Costa, with the fourth desk reserved for interns. Despite only seeing each other at work, Rachel, Costa and I had become good friends and often took a lunchtime walk together. Both were several years older than me and I appreciated their patience as I regularly asked them to explain the office lingo and how they managed their projects. In all, there were around forty of us on the second floor and in addition to the business section, there were teams that covered web design, market research, legal advice and management consultancy, all overseen by Ida, the office manager.

The third-floor office was a good deal more open and housed the senior staff, the most influential, and feared, of which was Greg, the commercial manager. He was a gruff, unyielding type who had a reputation for having little patience and frequently lost his temper. He had few friends in the office, bar a couple of middle-ranking toadies who would agree with his opinions with embarrassing enthusiasm. Greg was a master manipulator, acting friendly and gregarious in the open office or when he wanted something only to turn into a bully in the confines of a meeting room where his smile was soon replaced by a scowl. His toadies would excuse his behaviour with predictable soundbites such as 'he only wants what's best for the organisation' or 'he needs to be tough to get results.'

Before Greg had arrived, if any of the grant applications filed on behalf of companies were unsuccessful then we took it that there was good justification and the grant authority had prevented the launch of a business that was likely to fail. In any case, if feedback from the authority was taken onboard then another application could be made if the donor company so wished it. Greg looked at things differently, he thought every application should be successful the first time, every time. He was no fool, and through experience had learned what would make an application fly or fail. Having a successful template meant that he insisted that every application should measure up to it, come what may.

I had never understood why Greg was in such a position as he had little understanding of the details of what the second floor did and his abrupt manner had a demoralising effect on the office. Greg was more interested in making sure plans were adhered to, work was kept within timescales, objectives were met and grant applications succeeded. All this was unsurprising as it was suspected that his healthy bonus relied on such matters. Neither was it surprising that he ran the weekly Monday review meeting where applications were reviewed. The meeting was meant to give a chance for two-way communication but Greg used it as an opportunity to serve up criticism to whoever had come to his attention the previous week.

Any hint of delay was greeted with 'You're not pushing it enough' or 'I knew this would happen.' He would then belittle staff by elaborating on the mistake he felt had been made and questioning their competency, commitment or integrity. Greg was not one for giving out praise, even when the most stretched of milestones were met, such achievements were greeted with 'That's your job' or 'That's what I pay you for.' Myself, Rachel and Costa were always glad to get these thirty minutes of chest beating and bluster out of the way so we could get back to what we should be doing.

More frequent audits had not helped the sense of anxiety in the office. The audits were carried out by Alison from the Local Development Office, the place which approved grant applications and held the finances. To me, and despite her job, there was nothing inherently scary about Alison as, on one of her earlier visits, she had stopped at my desk to ask how I was getting on, having noticed I was a newcomer. She had been casually dressed, I thought, for an auditor, and wore a perfume with the most pleasing scent, a scent that, unlike people's names, I was unlikely to forget. Her snappy chat had intrigued me, and I'd hoped to catch up with her on one of her next visits. She even left me her card and said that if I ever needed help then to get in touch. Now, though, I dreaded the thought of speaking to her, such was my uneasiness about the grant application I was currently working on.

I inherited this latest job a few months back when Greg had invited me up to his office. He had been all smiles and gave me 'a gold-plated career opportunity' to work on one of his star projects, a start-up that was spun off from a local software company. He reckoned that with most of the figures and forecasts available, the application needed a finisher to get it over the line. Greg could see no issues as the management consultant team was happy with the preliminary copies of the documents they had seen. What Greg handed over was a very impressive-looking fifty-page dossier with all the buzzwords and an appealing sales forecast. The training and knowledge section was admirable, as was the marketing strategy and overview.

I was a finisher, but I was also a detail person and a worrier, small things bothered me. As I checked through Greg's application, I grew anxious. After some research, I realised that the local impact statement was overblown and the balance sheet predictions overly generous. Furthermore, a risk assessment that consisted of three lines did not inspire me with confidence.

When I pushed back, Greg argued in open forum that I was being overly cautious, not a trait that would see me advance in a progressive company like his. He declared that the application was in good shape when it was handed over to me and warned that I was getting a reputation for dropping the ball and not being assertive enough. When I asked for more time to do a decent job of the risk analysis, I was told that I was being pedantic, turning the thing into an epic or hankering for overtime. I talked to Rachel and Costa to find that Greg's behaviour with me was falling into a repeating pattern and I should stick to my guns. The general opinion in the office was that Greg needed applications to be turned around in four months as this was one stipulation for his bonus, at least, he had been overheard saying this was the case. My application was now close to the deadline.

Upon arrival, my body went directly to Ida and explained the circumstances of the weekend. He pointed out the cut to his head, which being above the hairline, and having healed somewhat, was not so noticeable. Ida was sympathetic to the point that she asked my body if he was okay to work, adding that there would be no problem if he needed to leave early. My body politely refused both options; he was being affable with no sign of the haughtiness that I had witnessed in the hospital.

After finishing with Ida my body started to set up for

the day at his desk and fired up his laptop. For Greg's 'career opportunity' application, I was waiting for the software company to get back with clarification on how many local jobs would be created, the application stated twenty but this seemed on the high side. It had been over a week since I had asked the question, and the delay in responding only added weight to my worry that the number was overblown. I was hoping an email would be in my inbox stating that twenty was good and with a justification. The desktop screen had still not appeared, courtesy of the usual Monday morning computer updates, when Rachel and Costa arrived. They stood aghast as my body relayed the events of the weekend and both felt I should be granted leave. My body assured them he was fine but as the conversation developed, he went on to say that he did not feel his usual self and had little patience. The conversation could have gone on if was not for the morning debrief, the office was emptying into the conference room.

"My computer hasn't fired up yet," said my body, "I'll have no update on Greg's star project, that'll please him. Oh well, I wonder what he'll say to that? He'll probably sack me."

"Don't even joke," said Rachel. "I hate the man. I just wish someone would give him a taste of his own medicine."

The rest of the office were already in the conference room as we reluctantly filed in to join them around the large boardroom-style table. A few minutes later, the room fell silent as Greg appeared in the doorway and huffed his way to his seat at the head of affairs. Greg's expression of irritation told me that this week's session was going to be no different to any other.

After a brief resume of company news, he started with his usual grunt about slipped milestones. The main beef this week surrounded an application that had been returned asking for more details for the business forecast. One of our colleagues, Pete, as the main author, was criticised heavily and sat staring at Greg in unsurprised indignation. What worried me more was that my body was also staring at Greg but with fiery, unyielding pin-point eyes. When Greg called Pete's application shoddy and commented that staff should spend less time making tea and more time doing the job they were paid for, my body stiffened.

"Who approved Pete's application?" he asked, knowing that it would have been Greg. I cringed as being confrontational was not my style, I agreed with what my body was saying, but I would not have said it in this meeting.

"I don't remember asking for an opinion?" said Greg, looking around at my body who was now the focus of Greg and his toadies.

"I'm giving it to you for free, who approved the application?" My body was not going to be put off

"That has nothing to do with it,' argued Greg. "It's the responsibility of the author to talk to the right people to get the appropriate facts and figures."

"Okay, so what exactly was it that caused the application to be rejected."

"The details are confidential, you know that." Greg was now angry but sensing danger, and the shutters were coming down.

"Rubbish, I'm only asking what caused the application to fail, not details, call it a chance to share learning."

"Shut up, Fred." Greg banged his fist on the table

causing his coffee to spill over the rim of its cup. He then went silent for a second before looking at his watch, I noticed his hand was shaking. “I’ve got an important conference call I must attend. Pete, you’re on the agenda first next week, I expect to see a full explanation of what went wrong and a fix. Col, you take the meeting from here.” And with that Greg got up and left, not bothering to attend to the spilt coffee. He turned back at the door and beckoned Ida to accompany him. It was a surprise that he had gone without even mentioning my application, probably a reflection of how rattled he was. Greg had taken flight, at least that’s the way it seemed to me.

Minutes later, Ida pulled my body from the conference room and insisted that he should take the rest of the week off on medical grounds. I sensed my body had lit the blue touch paper. Would things cool off after a week? I was not sure but felt that my general frustrations had well and truly risen to the surface. My body accepted Ida’s instruction and said goodbye to Rachel and Costa. They had both praised him for speaking up on Pete’s behalf but warned of the danger he was putting himself in.

I followed my body from the office and we were soon on the tram home. I reflected on my body’s behaviour with Greg, he had been brave but foolhardy. Was my job in jeopardy? Did I care? I did care – without that job, I would probably have to leave Nottingham and if I left Nottingham then I would leave Lou.

CHAPTER ELEVEN

At home, my body had made a cup of tea, opened another packet of ginger nuts and sat at the kitchen table smartphone in hand. He surfed from one website to another, adding items to respective baskets as he went, there seemed to be no pattern. 'What about looking for another job,' I thought, 'or updating your resume.' I stood worrying, I had built up a pot of savings for a deposit on a flat and a prolonged period of unemployment would eat into it very nicely, not to mention my body's sudden spending spree.

My flat deposit had earned just a few hundred pounds interest in the last year and would not afford me anywhere close to my current location, not that I had spent much time looking. Truth be told, I liked it here. I liked the area but more particularly I liked living with Lou. And that was the problem, I was in no rush to move out, despite telling Lou when I moved in, and I believed it at the time, that I would stay about a year while I found a place of my own. I was well into my second year now and no further forward in terms of finding my own place. Lou had never mentioned my extended tenure and neither had I. It was silly to think that I could lodge with Lou indefinitely but this is what I kind of hoped for.

And what would Lou think of my shopping spree, I had seen several fast fashion stores flash up on the screen. Lou always tried to buy ethically but particularly so when it came to clothes. She liked the idea of being a global citizen and had passed some of that on to me. Lou hated the thought of fast fashion and all it entails; we had watched a documentary on forced labour in sweatshops which was one of the only occasions that I had seen her with teary eyes. The thought that I had brought about a similar reaction with my practical joke involving the parking ticket still stung.

After finishing his tea, and half the gingernuts, he moved to the lounge where he switched the television on. He sat back, sharing his attention between the television and his phone, continuing to jump from one website to another. Simply sitting beside my body and watching his behaviour, trying to figure out what he was thinking, and what his next move would be was becoming tiresome. Moreover, I was finding morning television irritating beyond endurance. If I was in his shoes then I would have already started looking for another opportunity in the area, scouring the internet or even visiting the job centre. My body, however, seemed content to while away the time aimlessly.

Morning television trundled on, an interview with a man whose pet dog could speak a few actual words, an item on how to cook on a budget, then what was tantamount to an advert, autumn fashion must-haves. I winced, what was saved on food could be spent on fast fashion. None of this essential viewing had much effect on my body but the next item did, 'competition time.' The lure of a brand-new motor home, of all things, and a wad of cash sent him racing for his phone to text the word 'DREAM' to the number pasted across the screen. As he did so a thought occurred to me, was my body being influenced by the power of suggestion and that's why he had entered the competition, the announcer had virtually told him to do so, I think the words were, 'What are you waiting for? Enter now.' My mood lifted and I felt an excitement rushing through me, I had discovered something tangible, something I could share with Fang.

The adverts came on and my body turned off the television, went upstairs and started packing. I was confused, why was he packing? Where was he going? Why such a sudden decision? I reprimanded myself, I had not watched what he was doing on his phone before he had entered the competition, I had become distracted by the television myself. Had something on the phone prompted his rush of activity? I had no answers, but six, or so, pairs of socks and boxer shorts told me of the likely duration of his trip. Back downstairs, holdall bulging, he left the house, turning at the end of the drive to take a long look at the house, ominous I thought. He then set off with purpose and it was not long before we had arrived at the local railway station, the exact place where Fang and I had been separated from our bodies.

My body made his way to the platform for destinations away from the city where the next arrival was the train to Chesterfield. It struck me where he was heading, it was a route I had taken many times, change at Chesterfield for Darlington and a local train to his final destination; he was going back home to the North, probably to stay with my parents. With the train due in three minutes, I had a decision to make, follow my body or stay in Nottingham to meet up with Fang. It did not take long to decide; I was staying to meet up with Fang. In any case, I could always go back North to find my body at a later date.

If my body was going back home, what havoc might he wreak? How would he behave with my parents? What about old friendships he might tarnish or, then again, rekindle; I had not been good at keeping in touch. I had gone back to see my folks only a respectable number of times since moving to Nottingham and there was no denying that the frequency of these visits had dropped significantly since being at Lou's. The reason was simple enough; I preferred to stay with Lou. I prized the weekends we had together. I would help in the garden or with the decorating or with anything else that she asked for help with. And on occasion, we would visit the theatre to see a play of some relevance to Lou's curriculum or go to the cinema for the latest release. I thought about Lou's infectious sense of fun. She would often make some off-the-cuff comment and then, moments later, realise some irony to what she had said and burst into laughter. And if I made a silly remark, which I was prone to do here and there, Lou would always oblige me with laughter. It was intoxicating, and I think wanting to see her laugh had led to the excursion into practical jokes, though with the parking ticket I had gone too far.

Always at the back of my mind had been the thought that one day this cosy world which I had stumbled into would come to an end. Lou often had friends and colleagues over for dinner, to which I was always welcomed, but which sometimes depressed me as I feared that, from such a wide circle, she would soon settle with one of her many suitors.

And her circle was growing, she had recently won a regional award for her teaching which had seen her nominated for national recognition, it seemed the eyes of the nation were upon her. Now there was every possibility that my body would seal my fate for me, if he was heading home with his job in jeopardy, how easily could a week turn into two, or a month or a permanent move? How could I have imagined that my separation from Lou would come in such grotesque circumstances that faced me now?

The train arrived and my body duly alighted along with a handful of others. It struck me that I might as well swap platforms to catch the next train into the city to meet up with Fang. I made my way to the end of the platform and waited at the crossing, finding myself exactly where I had been standing when the lightning released me from my body. Between the opposite track and where I stood was a fresh patch of tarmac, about a foot square. I surmised that this marked the exact spot where the lightning struck and was a repair of the damage caused. I snorted a laugh, usually potholes and the like take months to get filled. And why didn't the lightning strike the track, or the train, or the barrier or any of the other metalwork around for that matter, surely the lightning would look for a conductor, it did not make sense.

As the train to Chesterfield accelerated through the crossing, I looked up to see the loom of figures behind the windows, and together with the blue smoke of the diesel fumes and the noise of the engine, my mind was transported back to the fateful night when lightning struck. I closed my eyes. A memory that must have been buried by shock started to return. I was seeing a face in the train window, illuminated by the lightning, the very last thing I saw before I was launched into the air, a serene face in the peacefulness of sleep, it was Fang.

CHAPTER TWELVE

It was nearly a quarter to five when Fang followed her body through the hotel doors and cast me a wide smile across the busy lobby. With her body setting off up the stairs, Fang threw herself into the chair next to mine.

I could hardly muster a hello, all thoughts eclipsed by the memory of Fang at the train window and the significance of the fresh patch of tarmac. Yet my friend was so full of enthusiasm and ready with a summary of how her day had gone, that I didn't get the chance to share my news. Fang explained that when her body arrived promptly at headquarters, they were not prepared. The spare desk set aside for her was piled high with defunct IT equipment and had to be cleared, her login details for the computer system were not available and her office buddy, Sally, had called in sick with a cold. After her resume, Fang sat back with a puzzled expression.

"Is this state of unreadiness typical of companies here?"

I paused for a moment.

"I think we sometimes forget what, or rather who, is important. We put important things off by allowing ourselves to become side-tracked and distracted."

"I'm important?"

"I'd have said so, they're lucky to have you. Their behaviour gives them plenty to apologise for, though I don't think it's done out of malice, more out of unintentional carelessness."

"Everyone was kind of apologetic and if Sally is still off ill tomorrow, then the office manager will stand in. In the meantime, I have been left with some light reading: printouts of the company's health and safety policy, their environment policy, their travel policy, their code of conduct and their IT policy."

Inevitably, Fang asked how work had been for me. I thought about glossing over the morning's drama but could be nothing less than honest. I told Fang about my continued worries for Lou, about the bullying Greg and the blow-up in the weekly meeting. And of how my body had suddenly decided to visit my home town, likely returning on Sunday. Fang listened intently, absorbing details, as was her habit. I was glad to get these things off my chest and when I had related all the essential details, I sat back. Just as I remembered seeing Fang's face at the train window, she jumped to her feet.

Fang had noticed the receptionist was retiring to the back room and we seized our chance to resume searching the internet. This time we typed in 'lightning' hoping to find a clue as to which of its effects could have blown our spirits from our bodies and therefore which might prompt our return.

We picked out an article that told us of a rare, and

powerful, form of lightning that originates from the upper parts of a cloud. In such a case, a single bolt can strike up to fifteen miles from the cloud, often away from any rain. I remembered that it had not been raining at the moment the lightning struck on the fateful night, the rain came later. And I remembered something else, I heard no more thunder that night, it was as if the full energy of the storm had been released in a single bolt of lightning.

Another article suggested that Fang had been right, what triggers lightning bolts was not precisely known. It theorised that lightning was due to the interaction of cosmic rays with ice crystals in a cloud which caused an avalanche of electrons to fall to the ground. This was just one theory, there were many more, all of which went over my head.

We searched on the ‘effects of lightning’ and scrolled through page after page of facts and hypotheses. Fang seemed to be absorbing the information and occasionally said a few words out loud, as if significant. I heard terrestrial gamma-ray flashes, X-ray pulses, ionising radiation and cosmic energy but which of these effects, if any, had expelled our consciousnesses from our bodies?

I had reached saturation point, not only was I not reading the text, my mind had locked up. I was feeling like the class dunce. Fang glanced at me, as she did habitually to check my expression, and this time she must have sensed my impasse and we stopped scrolling.

“We need to simplify things and look at it from another angle,” she said. “We think something in the lightning blew us out of our bodies, we think a dose of the same thing will get us back. That’s great as far as it goes but you know what I think is the real issue?" I shrugged my incomprehension. "What we are reading is earth science, and we need to think outside of that."

And on that note, our fingers closed the browser and we moved back to a pair of comfy chairs. I was relieved that we had called a halt to the research and sat back in relaxation, but Fang had a look of concentration as if wrestling with all the facts we had uncovered.

"What are you thinking?" I asked.

"I'm thinking that if we are spirits then why wouldn't we be in the spirit world?"

"We ought to be."

"So, and this is my real question, why haven't we seen other spirits yet?"

The same question had occurred to me, continually, but I had convinced myself it was just the nature of things. I shared my thoughts, glad that I could contribute after the mind-boggling science of electron avalanches and terrestrial gamma-ray flashes.

"Perhaps spirits don't hang around, if their bodies die then, presumably, they pass over to wherever they pass over to. Or, if they result from near death, like the guy on the internet, they are only spirits for three minutes or something."

"We should try harder to find another spirit, confirm were in the spirit world. If we find a spirit then who knows where that will take us, but it's got to be better than searching the internet. The question is where do we find spirits?"

"How about a graveyard?" It seemed an obvious thing to say but my second thought was that those spirits would have passed over already, I corrected myself and threw the question back to Fang. "Forget that. What do you think?"

"A place where you will find people who have just died, where there are seriously ill people in danger of dying, the hospital accident room or intensive care."

I hardly absorbed what Fang had said because my mind had not quite left the graveyard, not surprising as the thought had spooked me and my thoughts had turned to apparitions floating around dark, eroded gravestones.

"Fang, there is another thing, what about ghosts, aren't those spirits who have not passed over?"

"You're suggesting a ghost hunt."

"I guess I am, you did say to look at it from another angle, and there is no other country, I should imagine, that has more ghosts than the UK."

"Really," Fang sat back, "Tell me more about ghosts here."

Where science had failed to inspire me, I found the thought of searching for the presence of phantoms scary and captivating at the same time. Fang seemed to be finding the attraction of the ghoulish irresistible too.

"Not that I believed in ghosts before all this, but every town, every big house and every castle is haunted, allegedly."

"What about Nottingham Castle, we didn't see any there."

"We didn't, but there are stories, remember Mortimer's hole."

"I do remember now you mention it, Queen Isabella as well. Is there any particular ghost you think we should look for?"

"No, I mean, I'd not thought of it like that."

"A relative, maybe."

"I'd not thought of that either though there's nothing I can think of that would cause a relative to call from beyond the grave."

"Are you sure?"

The fact was I wasn't sure anymore, there were always loose ends when someone died, things that you wished you'd told them, things you wish you hadn't said or done. I was finding I could only be frank.

"Fairly sure, at least there's nothing that would warrant being jettisoned into the spirit world for."

"It can't be a relative of mine, I have none here. I still think the first place to try would be the hospital, if we chanced upon a death then we may find a fresh spirit. Are you okay Fred?"

Fang had spoken in all sincerity but the thought of watching someone die had rather disturbed me and my expression must have reflected what I was thinking, I could not deny it.

"The thing is, it sounds macabre waiting for someone to die."

"Well, there might be ghosts there too, have you heard of any at the hospital."

It occurred to me that I had and the story only came to mind when I had been asked the direct question.

"Now you mention it, a nurse who haunts the staff nap room, she taps the shoulder of those using the facility if she thinks they've overslept."

"Hmm." Fang cast a sideways glance then met my gaze. "Seek and ye shall find, that's the saying, isn't it?" I nodded approvingly. "That's decided then, you go home to Lou tonight then we hit the road for a lecture on out-of-body experiences tomorrow and after that, the hospital to look for spirits, old or new."

CHAPTER THIRTEEN

I arrived back home, the sky already dark, to see Lou's car on the drive. As the front room curtains were drawn, I made my way around to the rear. Light from the kitchen window dimly illuminated the back garden, half of which was given over to the cultivation of vegetables, and I saw a mound of freshly dug earth where the runner beans had grown so successfully over the summer. Their frame had been dismantled and some of the long canes were laid across the small patio though there was no sign of the plants themselves, presumably, these had gone into the compost bin.

I moved further into the garden and was relieved to see Lou happily occupied in the shed. From her muddy shoes, I realised she must have been catching up with the gardening and finishing off by placing the canes in the shed for winter, canes that I had bought and carried home in hazardous circumstances. One morning in early spring, knowing there was a DIY store close to my office, Lou had asked if I could get 'about a dozen' canes for a runner bean frame. Of course, I obliged but only to realise when in the store that Lou had not mentioned a length. Not wanting to get too short, I selected a dozen of the longest canes, which happened to be eight-foot. My thinking was that if shorter were needed then the canes could be cut down to size. It was a decision I soon regretted as it gave me a precarious journey home on the tram trying to avoid stabbing my fellow passengers as the untethered canes continuously slipped from my grip. By the time I got home, I must have lost a pound in sweat through the sheer worry of it all. To make me feel better, Lou used the canes as they were and, eventually, the runner beans reached the very top.

Now, though, she was having a tricky time getting all the canes into the shed. They just squeezed in but only if placed on the diagonal of the wall avoiding the tools hung on nails and slotting in behind the rack with paint pots, buckets and seed trays. As Lou manoeuvred the last cane into position, it caught the secateurs which fell from their nail and clattered to the ground. Lou cursed my name under her breath. Perhaps, she could see me after all, in her head at least, as she thought of her eager-to-please lodger who had brought home a dozen oversized canes.

Lou picked up the secateurs, which had fallen next to an old pair of shoes that I used for gardening, before hesitating, her eyes gleamed. She placed the secateurs back on their nail, picked up my shoes and took a couple of sheets of the newspaper that were used for the seedling trays. She then scrunched the sheets up into two balls, wet them under the outside tap, compressed them in her hands and rammed one deep into each of my shoes. I took Lou's prank as a good omen; she was thinking of me and, in a sense, this was business as usual. Once Lou had finished tidying up, I followed her through the back door into the kitchen.

As she stood washing her hands, I considered what I was doing and my nerve started to fail me. I was, after all, spying on Lou and I felt wretched about it. I steadied myself by remembering my purpose, to find clues as to what Lou thought of me and nothing else. I decided to act as if she knew I was there and if there was any doubt then I would confine myself to another room. I watched as she moved around the kitchen preparing and cooking a stir fry, all her actions perfectly mundane and normal. Lou played music from her phone as she cleared up, she looked content, happy, carefree even. She warmed milk in the microwave and then danced around the kitchen to collect a spoon from the drawer and a cup from the cupboard. An agonising thought came to me; no matter how well Lou and I had got along, I would not be missed.

With a cup of hot chocolate on the coffee table, Lou had settled in the front room to look over one of her scripts as she had done many times before. On occasion, I had helped by reading a part opposite Lou who would give me guidance on delivery and voice projection. I sat down on the settee beside her as she put on her reading glasses and flicked her hair behind her ears. She started reading through the script, making notes in the margin as she went with her biro that had three retractable points of different colours: blue, green and red. Lou continued making notes, occasionally sighing, occasionally smiling and occasionally clicking the pen to a different colour. Then at the end of each page, she would say the lines out loud, changing tone according to the character. Time was not dragging as it had when I had observed my own body, and I was content observing the script come to life. I just wished I could join in and help with the dialogue.

After about thirty minutes, she glanced at her watch, made one last set of notes and packed the script into her school bag. She moved to the mirror in front of the fireplace and began to untie her hair which had been held in place by her silver hair clip. The clip was oval-shaped with the fine detail of a floral motif and made from pure silver. It was one of the few pieces of jewellery Lou owned and was a family heirloom, passed down from her grandmother. Lou had jokingly warned me once, should I ever think of buying her jewellery that she had a skin allergy, anything with nickel brought her out in a rash, but pure silver, like the hair clip, would be okay, as would gold.

I stood to the side and watched her shakedown her hair as it fell away from the clip's restriction. She placed the clip on the mantle then swept her hair back with her hands and turned her head from side to side, as if considering whether to have a cut. Feeling too much like a voyeur, I thought of turning away but was transfixed and could do nothing but watch as she manipulated her hair from one style to another, intermittently pausing and crossing her eyebrows. And as she swept her hair back one more time, I realised that our evening together had not revealed too much of what Lou thought about me but it had brought home what I thought about Lou; I was head over heels and had been since we had first met.

CHAPTER FOURTEEN

I had awoken on the settee to see Lou securing her hair with the silver clip, one of the last things she always did as part of her morning routine. Soon after, I took a last lingering look at her as she reversed off the drive then I set off for the tram stop. I was early for my rendezvous with Fang for our journey to Loughborough and our much-anticipated lecture so stayed on the tram to the city centre where I wandered a little before heading back to the railway station.

I took up position on a wide wooden bench nestled under the platform canopy. It was a great vantage point to see the trains arriving and departing across the station. As passengers boarded, I wondered where they were all going and what the day had in store for them. As people passed close by me, it was their expressions that absorbed me most. I witnessed smiles of the content, frowns of the weary, the vagueness of those lost in their own thoughts and the purposefulness of the business-like. Settling into the bench, it was not long before I was wondering if there was a purpose behind the excursion from humanity that Fang and I had found ourselves on. If so, would finding a spirit point the way? I had not got any further with this line of thought when I spotted Fang. She had not caught sight of me and was walking along the platform in my direction. I watched for a moment as she weaved her way past other travellers, she had a natural sparkle lighting the path before her. When I judged her to be within earshot, I raised my hand and shouted out.

"Lou, over here."

Fang heard my call and looked directly at me with knitted eyebrows. I instantly realised that I had said the wrong name, which was a habitual trait of mine and I had suffered many awkward moments because of it. So acute was the problem that I frequently avoided using people's names altogether, though when this was not possible then I would find myself staring blankly at a person while my mind ran through a long list of incorrect names. It was hard to know which was worse, the long awkward silence or the animosity brought about by blurting out the wrong name.

My unfortunate trait had bothered me to the extent that I had sought an opinion from an acquaintance of Lou's, called Nyla, who had studied psychology. Nyla did not practice the discipline professionally but was only too happy to dispense advice to those who sought it. So entertaining were Nyla's responses that she had become one of Lou's regular dinner guests. Nyla had thought that, although my habit was a tiresome one, there was nothing to worry about. It was to do with the way that our minds work. She explained that our brains are made up of semantic networks that contain information about related people, places and things that we group together. When trying to remember something, the network is activated, but it is easy to pick the wrong name out of the pool. For example, a mother calling to one sibling is very likely to call the name of another or even the pet dog's name, which are often pooled in the same group. In such an example, the theme of the grouping would be affection or home. Furthermore, that's why it is so confusing when you see someone out of context, a work colleague on your holiday, or suchlike, you are confounding your semantic networks.

"Did you just call me Lou?" asked Fang, as she joined me on the bench and unknitted her brows.

From my conversation with the amateur phycologist, I knew exactly why I had recalled Lou's name when looking at Fang and could be nothing but frank about it.

"Yeah, I did, sorry about that, habit of mine, calling people by the wrong name, I mean. I've sought help about it, it's because my brain has grouped you and Lou, in the same pool, or semantic network to give it its neurological name. In the moment of trying to retrieve your name, I retrieved hers which must have been close to hand, as I just left her this morning."

"You seem to be taken with Lou?" Fang was looking at me with interested eyes.

"We're just friends."

"Really?"

"Really."

"Mm. Here's a thing, a test to see how much you like a person; can you say straight off, and without hesitation, ten positive things about someone?" I looked at Fang blankly who then offered encouragement. "Go on then."

"I like her hair, the way I can never tell what colour it is, whether it's light brown or dark blonde, sometimes there are flecks of red when the light catches it. I like it when she wears it long, then again, I like it when she wears it up, with her silver hair clip, which is very stylish. I like it when she's wearing her reading glasses and tucks her hair behind her ears. I like it when she twiddles the light strands that dangle just in front of her ears when she's working on her scripts, thinking of storylines."

Fang held her hands up.

"Wow, I'll stop you there, that must be about five things already, and you've not got off her hair. I presume you're talking about Lou?

I realised that Fang had not specifically asked about anyone; I had set off on my narrative automatically thinking of Lou. I started to feel a little defensive.

"Yeah, I'm her lodger, we've shared the same house for over a year, I'm bound to notice these things."

"Fred, you adore the girl." I could not deny it and eventually acknowledged Fang with a reserved smile. Life without Lou would be sorrowful. "So, you adore Lou, and I'm pooled with her, so you adore me," Fang teased.

I did not argue. With Fang as a friend on one side of the spiritual divide and Lou on the other, I had a lot to be grateful for. Even so, feeling a little self-conscious, I moved the conversation to more comfortable territory.

"How was your body this morning, in the office?"

"She's been quiet," replied Fang, "though working through her list of things to do efficiently enough. The computer access was sorted out and, you'll like this, she's been asked to do a presentation on her first week in the UK next Monday. I can't wait. Oh, and her office buddy, Sally, turned up and has offered to take my body out at the weekend in her two-seater sports car. And here's the thing, when Sally asked my body where she would like to go, she replied Matlock Bath, where, or even what, is that?

"Matlock Bath? It's a village in Derbyshire, the next county. It's set in a gorge cut out by the river Derwent, it's a popular tourist attraction. They call the place Little Switzerland because of the cable cars that run up to the top of the hill."

"Sounds great."

"It is. Fang, I've just thought of something. Matlock Bath, there used to be a ghost trail there, roundabout Halloween time. I've not been on it but a friend has, and she spoke of the old theatre being a magnet for ghosts. The one I can remember is the white lady who appears from the side of the stage. I even think the place was in the newspapers when some of the staff refused to work alone because of the hauntings. We could follow your body on Saturday and look for ghosts at the same time, kill two birds with one stone."

"You think?"

"Why not, as the dice have rolled in that direction?"

"We'd have to find a way to get there, we'd never get in the car with my body and Sally."

"We'll get the train, there's one from Nottingham direct, the area must send hundreds of day trippers there every weekend, as I said, it's a popular tourist attraction. The main car park for the village is right next to the railway station so it shouldn't be too difficult to find your body if we get the timings right."

"Sally said she'd pick my body up at ten o'clock from the hotel."

"In that case let's check the timetable, we have time

before the next Loughborough train arrives. Come on, the timetables are in the station concourse."

We found the time of a suitable train, the 9.41 direct to Matlock Bath and cemented our plans for Saturday. I was glad about this on many fronts, Matlock Bath was a place I liked anyway, having visited many times, and the chance to spend time with Fang and her body again appealed greatly. But most of all, the anchors that had held me to my body had loosened, his influence dwindling, and, for the moment, I felt the excitement of the unknown as I embraced the spirit world. Or perhaps, the spirit world was embracing me.

The intercity train to Loughborough duly arrived and we afforded ourselves seats in the first-class carriage whose confines were strangely reassuring. We relaxed into our surroundings and watched as city buildings were replaced by the back gardens and parks of the suburbs. As the train sped through the station two stops from Nottingham, the significance of the location hit me.

"Fang, this is the station where our adventure started. The crossing at the end of the platform, see just there." I pointed to the lowered barrier as it flashed by. "That's where I was standing when the lightning struck. There's something else, when I was getting the train to come and see you yesterday, I was at that barrier again and saw precisely where the lightning struck the ground. You see there was some damage to the road and the spot has been repaired with fresh tarmac.

"The thing is, well two things. First thing, a memory came back to me yesterday; at the moment the lightning struck I saw your face in the train window, you were asleep, isn't that amazing." As Fang considered my discovery, I continued my narrative. "Second thing, the lightning had hit the road surface on the crossing midway between us. Why strike the road when there are metal tracks right next to that spot and metal railings on either side of the crossing? I mean, doesn't lightning go for conductors? It doesn't make sense."

Fang paused, put her clasped hands to her lips, as if praying, and sat forward.

"It makes sense all right, if Zeus, or the like, threw the lightning bolt down that night."

"What do you mean?" I sat up myself.

"The lightning strike, it might have been meant to spirit us both from our bodies."

It seemed that I was not the only one who felt that we were in the midst of a spirit world, a world in which we were only beginning to see the possibilities in front of us, Fang felt it too. At least our conversations were becoming more and more celestial: the acceptance we were spirits, our thirst to find others and now the idea that the lightning strike might even have selected us. The rhythmic clatter of the train, as we sped through the countryside, served to stir my curiosity. One question above all others kept appearing in the forefront of my mind.

"Why would the lightning strike choose us?" I asked. "I mean there's certainly nothing remarkable about me."

"Maybe earthly skills aren't needed," replied Fang.

I considered her words and found the thoughts that I had left on the platform bench returning.

"Do you think we're here for a purpose?"

"That's kind of what I was thinking when I said the lightning was meant for us."

"But what purpose?"

Fang stared directly at me with distant eyes.

"It's as if there is something out there that needs our attention, yet we have no idea what it is. We can only keep looking for signs and follow our instincts. We can't waste this chance, even if at first it felt we were victims of the strike."

I sniffed out in a moment of realisation.

"Fang, you've just triggered a memory. Remember I told you about semantic networks, I got that from Nyla, she's a bit of an amateur psychologist. She comes to the house sometimes for dinner, as one of Lou's guests. Anyway, Nyla reckoned that we all need to find a purpose and some people do it by turning pain into gain. I forget exactly what we'd been talking about or who else was there, but the theory is that if you've been affected by a serious illness or injury or the like, then you become predisposed to help people who've been similarly affected. If we find other spirits then we might be able to help them and they might be able to help us."

"Totally. And Nyla sounds like a very good friend to have."

"She is, though she's more a friend of Lou's than mine." I sat back in contemplation and wondered if Nyla had ever fielded a question on the causes of out-of-body experiences. I bet she would have a plausible explanation to hand. The next time she came to dinner, if there was a next time for me, I would ask her. No matter, I felt a deal of satisfaction that with Fang by my side we had agreed on such a virtuous path. Would my ambitions have been so worthy if I had been left to my own devices? I was sure that my imagination could easily find ways to exploit my hallowed position if I let it. I shuddered at the thought, remembering Fang would not be by my side forever.

CHAPTER FIFTEEN

Coronation Hall was a traditional red brick building among a clutch of more modern college buildings on the edge of the town centre. At the entrance, one of the double doors was wedged ajar with the other displaying a notice for the talk. Inside, beneath a high ceiling, rows of stacking chairs were neatly set out on the herringbone floor. Grand portraits, presumably of old academics or notable alumni, adorned the side walls above oak wooden panelling that ran shoulder height around the perimeter. There must have been over a hundred chairs set out, with only about a quarter occupied, as it seemed the majority of people were happy to stand at the sides in cliquey groups with the odd loner hovering.

The audience was very varied by age and by dress, which ranged from smart through to bohemian, a mix of academics and enthusiasts, I thought. There was a general buzz in the air as people talked excitedly in anticipation. It seemed to me that a fair amount of the audience knew each other, and I imagined that many had met at previous, similar gatherings. At the front of the hall, velvet navy curtains drawn back and revealing a wooden stage gave the venue a touch of the theatrical.

The speaker and host were standing behind a wooden lectern with a laptop perched on top. A large white screen, pulled down from the ceiling at the centre of the stage, was already showing the title slide, 'Inside out? The Science of Out-of-body Experiences by Dr Emile Beaumont, The British Guild of Metaphysicians.'

At Fang's suggestion, we climbed onto the stage and scanned the room, it was not beyond possibility that among the eclectic mix of attendees lurked a spirit. Fang even shouted out for any spirits to join us on stage. Surveying the audience, we were interrupted by a loud banging that rang out through the hall. Startled, we looked around to see the host hammering a gavel against its block. The room hushed and those still standing moved to vacant chairs. We held back and when everyone was sat down, we took a pair of seats on the front row.

The host started by welcoming everyone and proceeded to introduce the speaker. Dr Emile Beaumont had taken an interest in out-of-body experiences over twenty years ago and after having had a patient describe, in very convincing detail, such an ordeal. Over the years she had collected over a hundred accounts that had occurred as a result of various traumas such as heart attacks, road accidents and drownings. She was a qualified psychiatrist and, as such, had made a scientific study of the whole subject with a critical eye.

Just as the host was about to hand over to Dr Beaumont, a gunshot rang out. The audience gasped in panic, a few had jumped up out of their seats and were standing while others looked around in confusion.

“Good evening, sorry about that,” said Dr Beaumont while revealing from behind her back a starting pistol with a haze of blue smoke swirling around the barrel. “It was a blank. Doubtless, you have heard of the idiom ‘jump out of your skin.’ This was first used in England in the nineteenth century to describe any person who had been scared to the extent that they literally 'jumped out of their skin,' dying and becoming a ghost. Nowadays, it simply means someone has had a nasty fright.

“I can see I made everyone react in some way but only a minority jumped to their feet, those of you who did have a predisposition to do so. Similarly, it seems that out-of-body experiences involve a certain predisposition in the patient, not everyone who has a near-death experience has an out-of-body, in fact, less than one per cent”

Myself and Fang looked at each other, we had both stood up when the gunshot rang out and the speaker now had our full attention. Dr Beaumont went on to describe how one of the most common occurrences in a near-death experience was visualising a tunnel of light, only an effect of a dying brain. She was well aware of the supernatural, even religious, notions, such as a floating spirit awaiting ascension to the spirit world, that surrounded the subject, and without a universally accepted theory involving neuroscience, she feared that the paranormal would be taken as the more likely explanation. Her extensive research had shown that out-of-body experiences can be explained purely by processes within the brain and without recourse to the supernatural. She described how metaphysical studies had placed phrases, printed clearly in large type, on high shelves in hospital wards such that they would be easily spotted from a position of elevation, and not once had there been a correct identification by a patient who had endured an out-of-body experience.

The main thrust of her talk was that during a trauma then normal brain activity is interrupted and, in certain predisposed individuals, their senses go haywire. Deprived of sight then the patient's senses of smell, touch and hearing take over, filtering into the subconscious. The visual part of the brain then assembles the information from other senses into images which are added to the data that the brain could recall of its surroundings. Her slides showed images from brain scans which had been captured during studies on lucid dreaming, areas where the brain was active were coloured red. It was surmised that these same areas, the areas of imagination, are active during out-of-body experiences and the talk branched into neuroscience, little of which I understood.

Dr Beaumont concluded by reiterating that there was nothing to suggest that out-of-body experiences are anything but processes within the brain. With the screen now showing 'Thank you for listening, any questions?' a spontaneous round of applause broke out. The host rose to his feet and pointed to one of the many members of the audience with their hands up. After several questions, which were disappointingly dull and related to neuroscience, the host picked out a middle-aged lady. She was one of those dressed on the bohemian side with a turquoise chiffon scarf and, after standing up, asked if Dr Beaumont was aware of the theory of spirit attachment which had gained momentum with some psychiatrists and didn't this give credibility that out-of-body experiences were real. A murmur went around the room.

Dr Beaumont told how, given the nature of the talk, such questions often come up and, yes, she had heard of the theory of spirit attachment. Dr Beaumont explained that she did not advocate this theory but, in a surprising departure from the hard science that had been the mainstay of her talk, would explain it due to the general interest in the subject.

The theory claims that consciousness is a phenomenon in its own right and not just the result of brain activity. Upon death, it is purported that the spirit, the embodiment of consciousness, chooses not to follow the renowned tunnel of light but leaves the body to remain on the earthly plane. There are many supposed reasons why this happens the most popular being a traumatic or unexpected death and the idea of unfinished business on earth. Once detached, the spirit can attach itself to another human being through a fractured soul, caused by a physical or emotional trauma. She added a qualification, if a spirit remains unattached then it is classed as a ghost, confined to the place where they met their death.

Supporters of the spirit attachment cite verified recollections of previous lives, prodigal skills and the occurrence of unlearned languages as firm evidence of attached spirits. However, the condition is also alleged to cause symptoms such as fatigue, irrational behaviour, addictions, physical illness and multiple personalities. The cure, in the psychiatric world, is therapy through a medium to release the spirit, in a similar way to exorcism practised in religious circles. Such has been the success of these treatments, with reported life-changing benefits, that they are seen as a form of complementary medicine, even if it is not universally accepted that an attached spirit was the cause. Dr Beaumont ended her answer by assuring the audience that she had seen case files of patients where spirit attachment was claimed and, in each case, concluded that other conditions could easily explain their symptoms. Dr Beaumont had given a very comprehensive answer, I thought, for someone who did not believe in such things.

Explaining that time had run out the host drew the session to a close and thanked Dr Beaumont for the reassurance that out-of-body experiences could be explained by brain activity and that we do not have ghouls walking among us. The talk had certainly given myself and Fang much to think about, it had also given us words to describe our condition.

“That’s that then,” I said, “we’re detached spirits or ghosts haunting the earthly plane.”

“In that case, I have an idea,” responded Fang. As the audience gave another round of applause, Fang led me up to the speaker’s laptop which was still projecting the ‘any questions’ slide. As the audience watched on, we wrote ‘Goodbye everyone’ across the screen and then shut the computer down. The clapping resurged; presumably, the audience thought that the computer taking on a life of its own was a set-up to create an element of mystery and a memorable note on which to finish, though not quite as memorable as the gunshot that heralded the start. Unaware of what Fang and I had typed and confused by the audience’s reaction, Dr Beaumont looked across at the screen, went back to the desk, wiggled the mouse and checked the power lead. She looked dumbfounded and cursed under her breath.

"Knicky knocky ido," said Fang, her delightful giggle entrancing me once more.

We made our way to the front of the stage to survey the dispersing audience. The talk had certainly left its mark; the room was buzzing.

"What did you make of the attached spirit theory?" I asked.

"It goes some way to explain why we're not seeing other spirits; they've attached to humans. But remember Fred, the theory itself is a human one and just like human theories on lightning it might not be right and there's no way of testing it. The whole field is ripe for speculation and misrepresentation. What did you make of it?"

Before answering, I paused momentarily as I considered Fang's summary.

"My mind's still whirling. Hey, the lady who asked the question, there's a crowd around her, should we listen in?"

We jumped from the stage and hurried over to find out that she was a medium talking about how she had discovered spirits in her clients, sometimes up to eight in one body. After helping the spirits leave the patient and pass over, conditions such as stomach ache, alcoholism and indecision had been alleviated. I started to think that there was no condition that the spirits would not get blamed for. As she handed out a business card it occurred to me that she was simply drumming up business and could be a fraud though her next statement almost convinced me that she was not.

"I feel a presence," she said. Fang and I glanced at each other, then at the medium. She in turn was looking from one to another of the half dozen people gathered around her, quickly studying each of their faces before moving on to the next. The thought that she could sense us was frightening and I was relieved when her gaze past straight by us. "Is anyone suffering from insomnia here?" A bespectacled man in his forties looked surprised.

"Yes, me," he said.

"I think the presence is emanating from you, do you have any other symptoms?"

Fang ushered me away from the small crowd.

"The bags under his eyes alone looked a sure enough sign he suffers from insomnia," she said, "it's a scam."

My initial enthusiasm for the spirit attachment theory was wearing off and Fang's summary on the subject was making more sense.

"Do you think spirit attachment itself is a hoax?" I asked. "I mean, Dr Beaumont certainly thinks so and there are obviously fakers who would benefit from people who believed in this stuff."

"Well, it has been accepted by some in the medical profession, and by many in religious circles, so there is an obvious desire that it is true. And remember, we're living proof spirits can be released from bodies so I'm keeping my mind open. Let's go back to Nottingham and to the hospital to try and find a spirit presence. Remember, the clock is ticking and we need to find some real answers."

CHAPTER SIXTEEN

We arrived at the hospital as afternoon turned to evening and in the resultant half-light, my fears of witnessing death had resurfaced. Fang buoyed me up by suggesting that if we found a spirit passing over then it would be far better for them to have friendly company when departing the earthly plane than do so alone. With our day out at Matlock planned for Saturday, we could in the meantime stay at the hospital. We started by touring intensive care, the high dependency unit and the heart ward, stopping at those who looked the most seriously ill and had their eyes closed. We spoke to such individuals thinking if they had passed or were about to they might hear us; no one responded.

For the few patients we found walking around, and on the off chance they were spirits, we spoke to them too and tried to make eye contact; again, no one responded. Prompted by the sound of distant sirens, we made our way to the emergency department where we spent the rest of the evening. By ten o'clock, having had no luck finding a spirit, and fearing either one of us could succumb to sleep, we made our way to the relative calm of the heart ward to spend the night.

When I awoke, I saw Fang in the morning sunlight which beamed through the dusty ward windows. The heart ward was on the third floor, and she was peering down intently at the view below. I joined her to see a steady stream of hospital workers and visitors heading towards the main entrance. Fang stared at me with an uncharacteristic look of exasperation, her elbows resting on the wide sill.

"Fang, what is it?"

"The people, do you notice anything?" I looked down again, this time my gaze moved from individual to individual but I could see nothing and no one out of the ordinary.

"Not really, everything seems normal."

"What about this?" And Fang held her hand out flat just in front of the window. I shrugged my shoulders. Then Fang pointed to a vase of flowers, bathed in sunlight, further along the sill. "Now can you see it?" As I pondered, Fang stared at me with encouraging eyes as she moved her hand back and forth. "Look."

Finally, the penny dropped; we were shadowless.

"Jeez, how did we not notice earlier? I guess spirits don't cast shadows." I put my hand across Fang's but still no shadow.

"I should have realised," said Fang, "it would have been a good way to look for spirits. Look at the people below and their long shadows, each one a living soul."

I sensed a degree of self-reproach was the reason for Fang's look of exasperation. I too felt slow on the uptake, a normal occurrence for me. I remembered watching

Fang walking towards me on the station platform before our train journey to Loughborough and how I had thought she had lit the path in front of her. I now surmised this was because everyone else had the loom of their shadow beneath them, even under a milky sky. In comparison, Fang had stood out with light, literally, beneath her feet. If we had missed the casting of a shadow then what else had we missed? We spent a good twenty minutes watching the comings and goings outside the hospital, over a hundred people passed below, and every one of them had a shadow.

As the morning routine checks got underway, our minds turned to the task of watching out for a spirit leaving its body and, to get a better vantage point of the patients as they were assessed, we perched ourselves on the nurse's desk at the front of the ward. There were three beds on either side, each containing elderly ladies, each looking frail. A cleaner appeared in front of us and as he swabbed underneath the desk, I swung my legs to the side. Fang was prevented from doing the same by a tall cabinet on her side and instead lifted herself onto the desk and then rose to her feet. As the cleaner moved on, I swung my legs back but Fang remained standing, I looked up to see her eyes were fixed on the top of the cabinet.

"We're in the right place to look for spirits," said Fang.

"We are?" I replied, curious as to what else Fang had discovered.

"Look up here." I climbed onto the desk to see that placed on top of the tall cabinet was a laminated piece of white card with 'SWEET DREAMS' printed across it in large red letters. "Here's the thing, it must have been placed up here as part of a study, like the ones Dr Beaumont spoke about. If anyone has an out-of-body and finds themselves looking down on the ward then this is the piece of verifiable evidence."

"And it makes sense they've placed the cards here; I should imagine these walls have seen a few near-death experiences."

"We should check the other wards we've been to, see if any others have phrases in high places."

We duly checked to find it was only the three adjoining heart wards that had the cards, in each case the phrase 'SWEET DREAMS' was used.

Inspired by Fang's latest discovery, for the next two days and nights we mainly paid vigil to the patients in the heart wards in our quest to find a released spirit. To make the most of our visit, we also followed some of the medical staff on their rounds and beyond, this not only took us to other wards but also told us who the most seriously ill patients were and, therefore, who we should pay close attention to. We explored the far corners of the hospital and came across three separate staff rest rooms where we saw staff resting but no sign of the spirit nurse. And we sat in the canteens, walked the gardens and even learned a little anatomy with a class of medical students all in the hope of picking up on the zeitgeist and a clue as to the whereabouts of spirits.

It was only on Friday, as our thoughts were turning to our weekend trip to Matlock Bath, that the events that led to our first true insight into other spirits began. Just before lunch, a porter with a wheelchair arrived in the heart ward and collected the nurse from behind his desk. Together, they approached the lady nearest the window on the left-hand side, the board behind the bed gave her name as Mary but we had learned that she preferred to be called Nora. The nurse explained to Nora that it was time for her appointment at the X-ray department. The porter carefully helped Nora out of bed and into the wheelchair though she seemed spritely enough and almost embarrassed by the assistance given.

About half an hour later the lady returned and the porter offered to help her back into bed. She waved him away as she lifted herself from the wheelchair and sat on the bed before swinging her legs up and then resting back against a stack of pillows. She did not look spritely anymore, it looked as if she had taken a turn for the worse due to her exertion; her eyes were in a fixed stare. The porter frowned and called the nurse at the front desk. The nurse rushed over and, after taking just one look, pulled the emergency cord next to the bed.

Within an unfeasibly short time, the bed was surrounded by medical staff, seven in total who must have rushed from offices close by and adjacent wards upon hearing the alarm. Fang and I joined them and slotted into a space at the foot of the bed. Nora looked ghostly pale and rigid, her condition sounded life-threatening. Were we about to see a spirit released? I was rooted to the spot as the medics went about their work, shouting instructions to one another. They started CPR and the lead doctor called for a defibrillator. As Fang and I stared, transfixed by the drama, among the shouting, I was sure I heard the words 'no heartbeat.' Fang was looking around the ward then moved to Nora's side.

"Sweet dreams, Nora," called Fang.

Moments later the defibrillator arrived and the first application was deployed. As everyone stood back, all solemn-faced, the lady's body jerked forward. Then a second application, Nora's body jerked again, this time the staff all puffed their relief, Nora had been revived. The adrenalin rush in the staff was palpable as they thanked each other and, one by one, they left the scene leaving the lead doctor and the ward nurse. The whole episode can only have taken two minutes and my mind was swirling with all the high drama.

"She's coming round." said the doctor. Nora's eyes blinked open, and the doctor gave her a few moments to compose herself. "How do you feel?"

"Dreadful, what happened?" said Nora in a shaky voice. She cleared her throat and beckoned for a glass of water.

"You had an arrest but you're stable now, do you remember anything?"

"Just that I started to get a pain in my chest and found I couldn't speak, the light from the window was so bright I closed my eyes, but then, then..." Nora hesitated.

"What was it? Did you feel short of breath?"

"I always feel short of breath, but it wasn't that. I felt myself floating from the bed, so grabbed the sides to hold myself down. It sounds mad, but I felt if I floated off then that would be the end of me so I held on."

"You did exactly the right thing, although what you experienced would have been akin to a dream, a hallucination. Your hands didn't leave your sides until you were revived."

Nora crossed her eyebrows and then took a sip of water from the glass that the nurse had handed to her.

"Is that so, well it seemed real. And there's something else that seemed real."

"Go on."

"I heard a lot of shouting, mostly things I would have expected in an emergency except someone, a girl, wished me sweet dreams, she even got my name right."

"Sweet dreams? I can assure you no one said that." The nurse nodded his agreement. "It must have been part of the hallucination."

The doctor's reaction seemed muted, defensive even, was she unaware of the words placed on top of the cabinet just yards away? I, however, was astonished, Nora had heard Fang. As the doctor moved the conversation on to more physical matters, I turned to my friend.

"What does it mean?"

"It means that Nora heard me," replied Fang, "or rather her spirit did. Her spirit must have begun its final journey only to be recalled by resuscitation. I think she was simply not destined to have an out-of-body, at least we didn't see her spirit. Maybe all her earthly business was complete and without the defibrillator, she would have passed peacefully away."

"If she had been destined to have an out-of-body then we would have seen her spirit as it left her?"

"That's what I think. Finding a spirit leaving its body seems more remote than it did five minutes ago, maybe Dr Beaumont was right, it's a rare occurrence. Maybe, finding a spirit that's already left its body will be easier. You were right Fred; we need to find a ghost. Tell me more about the white lady of Matlock Bath."

CHAPTER SEVENTEEN

So it was, on Saturday morning, Fang and I boarded the 9.41 from Nottingham to Matlock Bath on our quest to find a ghost. Such was the busyness of the train with day-trippers that we only found a pair of empty seats at the end of the last carriage. Within thirty minutes, the tree-lined ridge to the right of the track announced that we were within the Derwent Valley and fifteen minutes after that we were pulling away from our penultimate stop. It was here that I noticed a tourist sign which unexpectedly sent a nervous twitch through me, the sign simply read 'This stop for Cromford Mills.' Clear of the station buildings, the object of my anxiety came into sight across the fields of the valley floor, the dark, imposing sight of Arkwright's eighteenth-century cotton mills. Fang had spotted my change of expression.

"Fred, what is it?"

I took a moment, wondering where to start.

"Have you heard of Arkwright's Mills?"

"I know something of them, spinning frames, the start

of mass production." I was impressed by my friend's knowledge, but not entirely surprised.

"Did you know that they're over there?" I pointed to the famous landmarks, now converted into shops and offices.

"Wow."

"Amazing isn't it, the birthplace of the industrial revolution, right here in the countryside. It was the power from the fast-flowing River Derwent that was one of the reasons Arkwright put his mills here. But the so-called progress came at a human cost, there was a cheap source of labour here too. Workers were exploited, enduring long hours, poor conditions and low wages." I was aware that I was beginning to sound like a textbook and, as I spoke, I felt the injustice of how Arkwright had profited from human misery. Perhaps, Lou's principles were rubbing off on me more than I had realised or perhaps this was my spiritual side showing itself. My feeling of injustice soon turned to anger as I thought of the employment of children that the mills were renowned for. "It's a shameful chapter in our history, young children were employed in a dangerous environment. This alone marks Arkwright out as an exploiter, whatever the history books say about him being a father figure for industrialisation."

I was shocked at the passion with which I had spoken. Fang gave a sympathetic smile.

"Understand the past and you can shape the future."

I nestled back in my seat to let Fang's words settle upon me. Why had I got so worked up, was there something about those mills that was related to our strange circumstances? Or was I overanalysing things as usual, trying to find meanings that were not there? Then again, I could not remember having any particular aversion to mills as a human, so why the strong reaction now? Before I could think through the matter any further, the train began to slow; we had reached our destination.

Matlock Bath railway station had only one track and only one platform. The station building, with its gently inclined and overhanging roof, reminded me of an alpine chalet. Together with the cable cars running high above and steep slopes on either side, it was easy to see how the town had earned the nickname of Little Switzerland. The single platform created a mysterious atmosphere with thoughts of no return. The question was, did the historic town trap spirits as well as it did tourists?

As we alighted, along with the multitude of human visitors, it occurred to me that a country railway station might be a place where spirits lurked so before we set off for the old theatre, we walked the length of the station and peered through each of the panelled windows that looked out on to the platform. There were no spirits to be seen but our ghost hunt had begun.

The car park by the side of the station was already busy with queues forming at the pay station but, as expected, there was no sign of a two-seater MGT. By my calculations, we would have more than enough time to investigate the old theatre before Fang's body and Sally arrived so we set off along the river gardens. Within a couple of minutes, we found ourselves standing in front of the renowned theatre building set between the River Derwent and the main road.

The grand Edwardian Façade was somewhat marred by the drab painted walls which, pale salmon pink in colour, suggested a dubious attempt at rejuvenation some years since. The building's dominating feature was its huge gothic dome set upon the flat roof though despite this touch of grandeur the overall impression was one of decline. With its general eeriness, if anywhere in town was haunted then this old theatre stood as good a chance as any. The imposing blue wooden doors at the entrance were held back and an uninviting dark recess stared at back us. I doubt I would have gone any further had I been alone, such was my trepidation, but Fang was resolute and together we made our entrance.

Inside, and at a quickened pace, this was going to be a whistlestop tour, we made our way through the dimness of the entrance hall and found ourselves in a café. At least here, the tall windows provided plenty of light and the peppering of customers looked reassuringly commonplace. The modern counter, chairs and tables belied both the worn wooden floor that they stood upon and the black antiquated ceiling above. We left the café through another hallway to find ourselves in a large room, the auditorium. The place was deserted with some illumination coming from arched windows that lined the walls. At the front, the stage area was in darkness, all the darker courtesy of the black paintwork. We climbed the stairs to the stage to find no white lady waiting in the wings.

The upper floors were just as confounding as the downstairs, deserted long rooms with modern fixtures in deteriorating surroundings. As we made our way back to the reception hall, I felt a tinge of disappointment that our visit was proving fruitless, but only a tinge. Deep down, I was not surprised and with no enthusiasm to extend our search to the extremities of the ground floor,

I wondered if Fang was feeling the same.

"If you were a spirit, would you hang out here?" I enquired.

"Fred, I am a spirit and I don't think I would. You?" I blinked away my slip of the tongue before answering.

"Not somewhere eerie and empty like this."

"Where would you go?"

"I'd go where there's colour and life, where people go for pleasure, enjoyment, that sort of thing."

"A place of fun?"

"Exactly, a place of fun."

"You know what, maybe we've been looking at things in the wrong way. What if the stories of ghosts are just stories and those stories depend on creepy surroundings? Let's do things differently; let's find a place of fun."

CHAPTER EIGHTEEN

Back at the car park the two-seater MGT was parked up and there was no sign of Fang's body or Sally, my calculations had proved to be inaccurate. Feeling that surveying the area from a fixed point was the best way to locate her body, Fang suggested we stand at the elbow in the main road against the metal railings which backed onto the river and which gave us a fine view up and down the high street.

Bikers in leather jackets, carefree day trippers, extended families and young couples all jostled for position along the pavement in front of the row of shops. Looking upon the line of amusement arcades, fish bars, ice cream parlours and gift stores, all with brightly coloured facades, it felt like the sea and a sandy beach should be behind us rather than the river.

Just as we were debating whether staying put was, in fact, the best strategy, Fang's body appeared from a café with Sally, they linked arms as they sauntered up the high street and after a brief pause outside, they entered an amusement arcade. We crossed the road to join them, a pavement sign invited passers-by of all ages to come in and experience the excitement of a bygone age. Inside was an assortment of classic amusements including one-armed bandits, flick ball machines, a fortune-telling machine and a laughing sailor. *A place of fun*.

Sally and Fang's body were standing in front of a penny falls machine, happily feeding adjacent slots with twopences from a plastic tub. Fang seemed relieved to see her body in such good spirits, relief that rubbed off on me and I started to take more notice of our surroundings.

On the opposite side of the penny falls stood a girl wearing a red raincoat with a daisy insignia on the breast pocket. Her coat was distinctive and I had a feeling she had been on the train from Nottingham. Her red hair was swept back with a black band and dark-rimmed glasses gave her the air of a young student, though she could have been barely ten years old. She hovered a coin, clasped between her thumb and forefinger, over the slot and stared longingly through the glass to the plethora of twopences below. I followed her gaze to see a bracelet on top of a ridge of coins that were protruding from the bottom ledge. Surely, a few more twopences released into the slot and the bracelet would be hers. But why just stand and stare? Why not release the coin? With head still, the girl swivelled her eyes to the left as if trying to see behind her. I noticed another girl and a boy, both a couple of years older and a couple of inches taller, standing at the girl's back and armed with a tub full of coins.

The predicament was clear enough. This was the girl's

last chance to win the much-coveted bracelet and her rivals behind were poised to move in the moment she relinquished her position. I looked back to the bracelet; it was a rubberised clasp band with red letters spelling out BFF on a green background. I wondered if the girl was planning on giving the bracelet away if she won it, and who that friend might be.

The pair behind her were becoming impatient. The girl still hovered her coin in the slot. The look on the boy's face told me that he was not one for waiting and he made a comment, he was moving in. The face of the girl at the slot twitched as the boy tried to shoulder her out of the way. I felt compelled to help and rushed around the machine and placed my hand on the back of the boy's neck. He shivered then paused momentarily. Just then, a lady arrived by the girl's side and dropped umpteen twopences into the girl's spare hand. The lady had grey hair bobbing around a triangular face, which, through the lines, had a similarity to her young charge. The two youngsters behind withdrew. I felt immense relief, an odd reaction over such a trivial situation.

"Let's hope these get it Alaysia," said the lady, "it was the last of my change, there's only ten so place them carefully."

"Thanks, Gran, I will."

Alaysia waited a second before finally letting go of the coin with which she had so resolutely guarded the machine. Her eyes shone brightly as she watched the undulating paddles move the coins with the bracelet on top ever closer to the drop tray. She waited a few more seconds before resting the next coin against the slot and with tightened lips let go. The result was that a coin dropped onto the lower ledge and the bracelet teetered even more tantalisingly. As Alaysia hovered another coin over the slot, I feared that the way these types of machines worked that nine more might not be enough. Fang appeared by my side.

"This is a common problem," she said and banged her hip against the side of the machine. I joined in, not that I had much hope given our attempts on the vending machine back at the hotel, but after five or six nudges, and with Alaysia still judiciously feeding the machine, a glut of coins dropped and with them the bracelet. Alaysia's smile appeared as she grabbed the bracelet from the tray leaving her grandma to kneel down and collect the coins. As her grandma straightened herself up, Alaysia held out her hand, palm flat out with the bracelet on top of it.

"For you," she said.

"Oh, Alaysia," replied her grandma, I hadn't realised, I thought you wanted it for yourself."

"No, I wanted it for you. BFF – best friends forever."

Grandma was not going to argue and obligingly fastened the bracelet around her wrist and showed Alaysia the result.

"Come on, let's get to the cable cars."

It was at this point that I noticed Fang's body and Sally had left, it struck me how preoccupied I must have been.

"Sorry Fang, I got a bit wrapped up. We should catch up with your body."

"Do you know what, I like the sound of a ride in a cable car, what do you think?"

"Don't you want to follow your body?"

"She seems happy enough. Should we follow these two, to the cable cars?"

"That's fine with me, it sounds like...fun." A ride in the cable cars appealed to me but so did following Alaysia; there was something about her that I liked, an affinity. Perhaps, she reminded me of myself when I was her age, is that why I had felt so compelled to try and help her? Perhaps, it was just me and I would have rushed to help anyone. We left the arcade and followed the pair to a newsagent a few doors down. Fang and I waited as they went inside. Outside, there was a stand with newspapers on display, one or two of the headlines seemed to have caught Fang's attention.

"What are newspapers like in Britain?" she asked. I snorted my contempt.

"We have a saying, don't believe anything you read in the newspapers," I said before adding with my deadpan face and having watched several passers-by eating chips from their wrappings. "In fact, unsold newspapers were at one time used as wrapping for takeaway fish and chips, that is until the 1980s when the fish and chip shops refused to use them, such was the decline in journalistic standards. Instead, they produced their own newspaper called 'The Daily Catch' for the purpose."

"You're joking, of course?" said Fang. I nodded.

"But the fish and chip shops have moved to printed greaseproof paper with that title, made especially for chip shops. They stopped using traditional newspapers because of health and safety reasons, toxic chemicals in the print, I think. Look here." I pointed to a passer-by, a biker, who, very obligingly, was holding a packet of chips with an example of a greaseproof paper design.

By this time, Alaysia had emerged from the newsagent, handing a puzzle magazine to her grandma who slotted it into her handbag. We followed as they crossed the road to the cable car station. Soon after, the four of us were safely aboard a cable car as it rose high above the bustling high street and into the low cloud that had settled over the gorge.

Once alighted at the top of the hill, we continued to follow Alaysia and her grandma and found ourselves in a gift shop dedicated to geology with an impressive selection of rocks, crystals, semi-precious stones and ubiquitous small bags of iron pyrite. As Alaysia marvelled at a display of crystals glistening in showcase lights, Fang and I looked over the exhibition which described the history of mining in the local area. Storyboards told of how different types of rocks were formed and how they can be dated using the radioactivity they emit. Moreover, lead ore, a mineral mined on site, is one the most radioactive rock types though, fortunately, in this regard, it is harmless to humans, good news for the old miners and modern visitors. Nevertheless, thanks to the presence of lead ore, the background radiation in the gorge is far higher than in the surrounding area.

Directly after the shop of rocks, Alaysia and her grandma joined a queue of around thirty people outside the entrance to a tunnel, we were about to embark on a tour of the underground caverns. With everyone equipped with safety helmets, the tour guide began her introduction.

"The main cavern in the hillside is three hundred and fifty million years old," she said. "The ground beneath us is riddled with former lead and fluorite mines, we'll use the tunnels the miners have left behind to reach the natural caverns." With a grave face, she added. "There are a few places where the roof is low and the lighting is only dim so mind your heads. Single file and hold on to the handrail where possible, the steps are uneven and can be tricky for even the strongest of walkers. It's one hundred and ninety-nine steps down to the main cavern. Follow me, we'll stop at a small cavern about halfway down."

Off we went, tagging on to the line of visitors who were cautiously descending into the dimness. I positioned myself by the side of Alaysia with her grandma and Fang directly behind us. The tunnel wall was damp and patches of green moss appeared around the occasional wall lights that illuminated the way. After well over a hundred steps, we reached the small cavern which, with a relatively flat floor and high ceiling, accommodated the group comfortably. The guide stopped and asked if everyone was okay, which everyone was. After talking about the geology of the area she issued a further warning, this time to watch out for the ghosts of dead miners that were said to roam the main cavern. As we descended more steps, Fang made an observation.

"Ghosts really are a British obsession, one that is not in the guides."

"Doesn't Singapore have ghosts," I responded, looking back towards my friend.

"Ghost stories are popular, but we have nothing on this scale, the whole place seems to be overrun by them." Fang narrowed her eyes. "Mm, overrun by stories that is. Do you think there'll be any ghosts waiting for us in the cavern?"

"You never know, but I'm predicting nothing since..."

I did not finish my sentence as a sudden vagueness came across me, the dimness had turned to darkness. I tried to shout Fang's name, but it was too late, I was just a ball of thought without the ability to move independently. I felt myself falling through blackness at an ever-increasing rate with no reference point other than the feeling of my speed of descent, then I stopped, then nothing.

Before I had the chance to worry further, I saw the faintest blue glimmer coming towards me which, as it got closer, became a shimmering mist of light and dark blues. As the outer edges of the mist reached me, I was pulled forward into its depths. And then I was back in the tunnel, walking up the steps with a line of people in front of me. But my movement was involuntary. I felt euphoric; I could feel a heartbeat, hear breathing and even smell the musty dampness of the cavern. I could see a hand stretched out from a red sleeve in front grabbing at the rail. I jostled with my memory; I had been wearing my navy hoody, where had the red sleeves come from? The hand at the rail seemed too small. I was looking at the world through a pair of spectacles, was this why my sense of perspective seemed a little odd? Then I had the realisation, I was attached to someone's body, a child's body, it was Alaysia.

CHAPTER NINETEEN

We were already back at the small cavern and there had been no sight of Fang, what had happened to her? Then again, if I was attached to Alaysia, had I lost the ability to see spirits? I was overcome with worry. I needed to go back and find Fang, but I was a mere passenger and Alaysia had already started climbing the remaining steps back to the cave entrance. Then, in that moment of strong emotion, the blue mist again and Alaysia appeared in front, as if she had passed right through me. Gone was the heartbeat, the breathing and the musty smell, I was back as my spirit self. I looked around, my heart leapt, Fang was at the other end of the small cavern, looking down into the depths of the tunnel leading to the main cavern.

"Fang." Her name had just burst from me, and I was almost embarrassed by the vigour with which I had shouted. Fang turned and on seeing me blinked in surprise, or more likely shock. I started to move towards her.

"Stay exactly where you are," she shouted back before hurrying towards me. "Fred, thank goodness, I've never been so relieved, I thought I'd...." Fang stopped mid-sentence and puffed her cheeks out. I wondered what she had been about to say in such a state of excitement. I did not ask, being more concerned by her heightened emotion.

"Are you okay?" I asked.

"Never mind me, are you okay, what happened?"

"Me? I'm fine," I replied coolly. Fang looked at me with scrunched lips, an expression that told me that she wasn't convinced by my answer, and neither was I. "No, not really. I feel dazed not to mention claustrophobic."

"Right, let's get out of here. You first and don't stop till we're in the open air. Go."

I did not have to be told again, such was the urgency in Fang's voice, and we soon found ourselves outside the entrance to the cave where the tour group were dispersing. Thoughts about what had just happened came so thick and fast that I barely knew what to say. For once, Fang looked as lost for words as I was. I spotted Alaysia, resplendent in her red coat, handing her helmet back to the guide and one thought rose above all the others.

"Fang, remember spirit attachment?" Fang's eyes beckoned. "I think I've just experienced it. I was attached to her, Alaysia, I mean, just for a few moments, but I was definitely attached."

"Fred, hang on, you were attached to Alaysia?"

"Yeah."

"For a few moments?"

"Yeah."

"Where were you for the rest of the time?"

"The rest of the time?"

"Fred, you were gone for around twenty minutes."

"That's impossible." I paused in confusion. "I'd assumed the whole experience was as brief from your point of view as it was from mine. Twenty minutes, what happened?"

"You just faded in front of me, one second you were by Alaysia's side and the next you were gone. I grabbed the air where you had disappeared to try and pull you back. I went down a few more steps still grabbing at the air, still hoping I might be able to rescue you. Then I saw the danger of the situation so moved back to the small cavern and waited."

"Danger?"

"That I could disappear too. All the time I was trying to pluck you from thin air, I was asking myself why you had disappeared and I had not. Then it came to me, proximity; my body is in the valley somewhere while yours is many kilometres away.

"About two hundred, if he's in my hometown."

"Precisely, a kilometre versus two hundred. This is the thing, what if the life source that kept you going had been stopped? Stopped by the depth of the rock and the physical distance your body was from you. Do you see what I'm thinking?" I shrugged my shoulders. "Our life source is still our bodies." I paused for a moment to let Fang's assertion settle upon me. "It's a bit like a mobile phone when you go through a tunnel, the signal will get weaker until you end up with no bars."

"Fang, I get it, distance above ground could diminish the source but being a hundred, or so, metres into solid rock would extinguish it."

"That's right, when I realised this, well it might have

been only a few more steps, a few more metres of rock, and I would find myself in the place where you were. I thought about taking those steps but didn't. I wouldn't have been any use to you, even if I had joined you."

"Joined me, what do you mean?"

"Fred, you'd lost your life source." I began to see what Fang was leading up to. "In those twenty minutes, you were dead."

CHAPTER TWENTY

Fang's grim assessment had taken me aback, if it was correct then I knew what death was, absolute nothingness, yet primed for another chance of life. And consequently, I had also experienced what it was like to be reborn, the wonderment of a first breath and a heartbeat through Alaysia. And the reason for Fang's frantic reaction when I had reappeared became clear, she had feared that I would not be coming back. I was grateful for her emotion, hoping it demonstrated her affinity for me.

Thinking about it, the loss of twenty minutes made sense. When I had disappeared, the tour was heading towards the main cavern yet when I joined Alaysia, moments later, the tour was returning from it. I had not quite grasped what was happening at the time but something that should have taken a full twenty minutes had taken seconds. I tried to think about what had happened in the missing time but nothing came. It was a void. Nevertheless, I was back with Fang and with the return of my composure came new questions; what caused me to attach and why of all people had it been Alaysia that I had attached to? I had certainly felt empathy, that is why we were following her in the first place but this did not explain the what and the why. As expected, Fang was full of curiosity too.

"If you attached to Alaysia," she said, "then we need to keep following her, come on." Having left the mine entrance, Alaysia and her grandma were making their way into the nearby café, Alaysia skipping and looking none the worse for my intrusion. We started to follow with Fang hurrying me along.

"Fang, I agree, but what is it?"

"Remember Dr Beaumont's lecture, that spirits can attach to those with fractured souls caused by a trauma." I stopped in my tracks, Fang turned to face me. "All I'm saying is there may be some trauma in Alaysia's life, this may have been the reason you were able to attach. I'm not sure but we should at least try to find out and see if we can help. After all, Alaysia rescued you, whether she knew about it or not. And here's another thing, we have found a facet of the spirit world, we can't walk past this." My friend had made some excellent points, and as she set off again, I followed without question.

We made our way through the restaurant entrance and joined Alaysia at a window table as she waited for her grandma to return from the serving counter. I felt comforted by the presence of Alaysia, more so by the tune she hummed while tracing her finger around a maze in her magazine. It seemed appropriate she should be doing this as Fang and I sat beside her trying to make sense of our own maze of facts.

"Tell me, what exactly do you remember when you disappeared?" said Fang.

I told her of the sequence of events. How I had felt vague, about falling in darkness and of the blue mist that had enveloped me just before I had found myself attached to Alaysia. After my brief explanation, Alaysia's grandma returned. Her swollen fingers grasped a tray with a pot of tea, a milkshake and two large slices of chocolate cake.

"We need this after all the steps we've done today," she said while setting the items on the table and, having taken a seat, began to delicately slice her piece of cake into small lumps.

"I've never felt so hungry," said Alaysia. I smiled at her wide-eyed expression as she struggled to fit the cake in her mouth, turning the slice sideways before eagerly biting off the nose. Fang, who had also been watching on with amusement, leant forward with urgency.

"Fred, I've just realised something, we are definitely getting our life source from our bodies, this is a drain on them."

"What do you mean?"

"As strange as it sounds, I think we're been powered by our body's minds. We need a connection and we need energy. The reason my body has been snacking on chocolate is that she needs the extra fuel, her mind is in overdrive doing all the extra thinking for me. Remember the article we read that said it takes twenty-five watts to run a mind, our bodies are running two."

I beamed; the fact that a mind required so much power, more than enough to illuminate a light bulb, still amused me. Furthermore, our research on the hotel computer was beginning to pay off.

"But wouldn't our bodies realise and try to communicate with us?"

"Not necessarily, this could be happening in the deep subconscious."

There was a ring of truth about Fang's latest assertion.

"My sudden craving for gingernuts, it's the same thing, my body needs the extra energy too. And that's why we sleep when our bodies do, their minds shut down. Fang, it fits together."

"Exactly, it fits together, though we still need to understand how all this could help us get back inside our bodies. That's where we need to focus some effort. Of course, I really will have to go back to Singapore with my body, ten thousand kilometres of Earth's crust would surely sever the connection. We have a week left together."

"But at least we're getting some cards in our hands, thanks to you." And it was thanks to Fang, we had been presented with the same information and I was making little of it, Fang was joining the dots for me. I was not surprised at this as I tended to be slow on the uptake. On occasion, it could be hours or days after an event that its true significance would dawn on me. Similarly, if Greg or one of his toadies made a snide remark at work then I would be left lost for words and it would only be much later, perhaps staring into space on the tram home and when the opportunity to regain some pride had gone, that I would think of a riposte. Nyla had surmised that my delay in connecting events showed that my subconscious was smarter than I was, and she wasn't joking. She reckoned that the hidden power of the subconscious is still one of the great challenges in philosophy. What has become clear is that the subconscious mind has more sophisticated abilities than most have thought and which no amount of research will reveal. The question was, would those abilities run to powering a remote spirit? On the evidence of Fang and I, it would.

Fang gave me a resigned smile.

"You know what, with the amount of thinking I've been doing then my body is probably in some shop getting chocolate. I better give her a break, let's just follow Alaysia and her grandma for the rest of the afternoon."

"Just like happy families," I said. Fang rolled her eyes.

"Remember though, look out for something that could be the cause of trauma for Alaysia, we owe her some help."

"Agreed and I owe her a life, she saved mine."

CHAPTER TWENTY-ONE

After a trip back down in the cable cars, Fang and I spent some time in the river gardens, delivering on our promise to stay with Alaysia and her grandma. So intrigued had we become by the affair in the caves, and so determined to help with any trauma, we decided to follow them home. This, as it turned out, was not too much of an inconvenience as they caught the Nottingham train and my feeling that I had noticed Alaysia on the outbound train was vindicated.

Having alighted at Castle Meadows, the stop before Nottingham, we walked for around ten minutes to find ourselves in front of a respectable semi-detached house with a tidy terraced garden planted with shrubs and roses. A short path sloped up to the front door on the side of the house. Inside, a hall led through to a lounge on the right and a kitchen to the left. With her coat off, Alaysia settled in the lounge, conscientiously tackling a word search from her magazine. Her short-sleeved top revealed a streak of faded-purple skin, just above her right elbow. My first thought was that I was looking upon an old injury, but my alarm soon passed as I realised it was nothing more than a birthmark. Fang had seen the discolouration too, although, like me, as soon as she realised its harmlessness, moved her attention to our surroundings.

The lounge was as neat and respectable as the outside of the house with a couple of shelves above a television on one side of a white marble fireplace and a tall, glass display cabinet on the other. The top shelf above the television housed mainly ornaments, which included a figurine of a lady in prayer, while the shelf below contained books of various sizes arranged from largest to smallest, left to right.

"Nice place," I said. Fang nodded.

"Hmm, she could well live here, with her grandma," she replied, "there's not even a photo of what could be a parent, look." Fang pointed to a row of three framed photographs on the wall to the side of the window: one of Alaysia with her grandma and two smaller ones of Alaysia alone, both school portraits.

"It must be tough, living apart from her parents, if that's what's happening. Do you think that could be the trauma?"

"It's possible, particularly if there was some abandonment. She seems content enough with her grandma, but who knows what she's feeling inside." I felt a twinge of guilt having shared Alaysia's mind, albeit for only a brief period, and learned nothing in this direction. I walked over to the photos to take a closer look. All of them showed Alaysia without glasses, and what appeared to be the most recent portrait caught my eye.

"Fang, I'm getting a sense of deja-vu."

"What do you mean?"

"I recognise her."

"Come, I clap for you." Fang applauded ceremoniously. "We've been with her half the day, it's Alaysia, without her glasses." And with that, Fang chuckled.

"I know. I mean, she reminds me of someone else. The dimpled cheeks, the light blue eyes..." my sentence tailed off as I drifted into a backward sweep of memory. Then, the sudden realisation. "Fang, it's the girl in the portrait at the gallery, the girl in the yellow dress."

Fang's eyes narrowed as she scrutinised the photo, and I felt a sense of satisfaction when I saw the moment that she made the connection too.

"You're right, at least they're remarkably similar."

We both looked back at Alaysia.

"What a coincidence."

Fang gave me a sideways glance and scrunched her lips in my direction, an expression which told me of her mounting curiosity and that some questions were about to come my way.

"Coincidence, you think so?"

"Why not?"

"Think about it, we are spirits free to roam anywhere and we end up following a girl who you attach to, and who probably saved you from oblivion, only to find she is in the image of a portrait from the gallery, a portrait we particularly stopped at and admired, defended even. We're either mistaken about the likeness, or there is more to it."

"But it all seems so completely random."

"Is it though?"

"Well, we just happened across Alaysia, and the

portrait, for that matter."

"Not so much happened across, in both cases we came across them when following my body. And once beside them, and in both cases, it was you who was, how should we say, drawn to them."

"I suppose." Though there was no supposing about it, Fang was right, she seemed to have a thread in her hand that was suggestive of the hidden depths of a spirit world we knew so little about. Had there really been some otherworldly intervention on that fateful night we were struck? Had some invisible force been guiding us throughout? With only a few dispersed pieces of the puzzle within our grasp, it was no easy matter to think through what image was forming, at least not for me. "Fang, what do you think is happening here?"

Fang turned to Alaysia then back to me.

"I'm not sure, you seem to have a finer sense of it than I do."

"What do you mean?"

"It's like I said, you seem to be the one that was drawn, to both the portrait and Alaysia. As the first case was the portrait, that might be the most important, think, what attracted you to it in the first place? Be completely open, the slightest detail might be important."

"I suppose I just liked it." Fang scrunched her lips again; she was expecting a lot more. I obliged. "I liked the artwork, the image was lifelike, as were some of the other portraits for that matter. I guess it was the girl's face, her blue eyes, dimpled cheeks and curls of red hair in front of her ears. The portrait stood out, at least, it did to me."

But if there was one reason above all others, what

was it?" I paused as I remembered back.

"Fang, something occurs to me, when those toffs made their vacuous remarks, I started to feel emotional, that's when it got personal."

"Personal?"

"Yeah, a feeling of protectiveness, I had the same feelings when I first saw Alaysia in the arcade. I was glad when we followed her, it felt as if we were guardian angels. I may have subconsciously recognised her similarity to the portrait."

"You felt protective?"

"Yeah, for sure."

"Then there are two links to find. One between Alaysia and the portrait and one between you and the portrait.

"Are you sure it's not a coincidence?"

"I don't like coincidences, dig deep enough and they reveal unexpected truths. It's the truth that might help us find a way back. I can't help thinking if we can figure this out then we'll be one step closer to knowing how to reattach, you did attach to Alaysia after all. There must be something about that painting, we need to go back and take another look. Did you read the captions with the children's portraits at the gallery?"

"No."

"Nor did I, that's the first thing we should do. I tell you what, let's have a good look around the house and see what we can find that would link Alaysia to the gallery. While we're looking, see if we can find any sign of a parent. We may be locked in until tomorrow anyway so it's a good use of our time. We need to think about when we can go back to the castle."

We started our search with the shelves over the

television and after a cursory examination of the ornaments we scrutinised the spine of each book. We moved onto the display cabinet, tall and white with doors of smoked glass. Peering inside we could see boxed games, a few more books, art materials and a small basket filled to the brim with letters.

"Dinner's ready," called Alaysia's grandma, "it's your favourite, fish fingers. Come and get it." We followed Alaysia to continue our search in the kitchen. Alaysia and her grandma dined at a small, round table which was set back from a single glass panelled door that opened onto the back garden. More letters were huddled in a letter rack on the window sill above a worktop and the haphazard way that they had been bunched allowed us to see many of the letterheads though none stood out as remarkable.

We turned and scanned the rest of the kitchen. Just above the radiator was a corkboard upon which was pinned a watercolour on white paper and in the unmistakable style of Lowry. On closer inspection, there was little doubt that this was a purposeful attempt to imitate the great northern master. A multitude of delicately painted matchstick men, women and children, resplendent in clogs, walked in front of a red brick mill and in the background a tall chimney belched smoke into a milky sky. A cluster of people, characteristically with no shadows, were gathered by the factory gate. The figures were huddled and crooked as if in some great lament. The bottom of the painting was signed by Alaysia and beside it was a page cut from a school report which stated, 'Alaysia has a vivid imagination and passion which comes over in her artwork, she has a rare talent and should be encouraged.'

"You know about Lowry?" I asked.

"Oh, yes," replied Fang, "Matchstick men. This looks like one of his paintings."

"You're not kidding, it's so good."

"Hmm, vivid imagination, I said that about you remember?"

Fang's comment brought a smile to my face as I recalled the afternoon in the castle grounds, laying side by side and spotting clouds that looked like animals.

"I remember. Come on, let's keep looking for a link."

The corkboard showed little else of interest, just a few business cards, a reminder for a dentist appointment and a calendar with scribbles, which we could make little of, against several of the dates.

"Get yourself a cookie," said Alaysia's grandma. Alaysia, who had already cleared her plate, walked over to the worksurface and took off the lid of a tall, round biscuit tin. She plucked out a homemade cookie which had been decorated with a smiley face in red icing and re-joined her grandma at the table.

Having exhausted our search of the kitchen, we moved upstairs to Alaysia's bedroom. It was a compact room, only twice the width of the bed, and nothing seemed out of the ordinary. A bookshelf crammed with story books, a multitude of soft toy animals resting against the headboard and a signed poster of Nottingham Forest Women F.C. on the wall all suggested that Alaysia was well established in her grandma's house. There was no sign of personal photographs and only a nightlight adorned the bedside table. We moved onto her grandma's bedroom which was dominated by an elderly-looking double bed with a black cast iron frame. A set of antique pine draws was topped with a circular, embroidered lace mat upon which stood two photographs, both in black and white and both in oak surrounds. The first was a portrait of a woman perhaps in her twenties with hair reminiscent of the 1940s and the second of a bride and groom on the steps of a brick building. I wondered if the bride was Alaysia's grandma but the photo was a touch grainy and it was difficult to detect any resemblance. The single portrait showed a passing likeness to Alaysia, I felt sure it must have been a relative but not her grandma and too old to have been her mother. After a cursory look in the bathroom, we made our way back down the narrow staircase. Our search of the house had yielded no sign of a parent, no evidence of trauma and no links with the castle gallery.

As the skies outside darkened, we returned to the lounge and propped ourselves up against the wall beneath the window to observe Alaysia and her grandma, who had nestled into the sofa to watch the usual Saturday night television fare. We listened for any snatch of conversation between the two that might help in our quest for information. My mind was turning over and over, trying to think what could link me to the portrait at the castle gallery but it was hopeless, there was nothing. And what of the trauma we thought might have afflicted Alaysia, what could that be?

I had succumbed to sleep and found myself waking, in the morning light, to see Fang with her hands clasped in front of her, index fingers pointing up and touching her lips.

"Morning Fang," I said. She smiled her acknowledgement; I took it she was deep in thought and turned my attention to Alaysia who was sitting in the armchair with a sketchbook. By her side was a tin of around twenty colouring pencils, neatly arranged by colour. Standing up to look, I found myself doubting what I saw appearing on the page. I was transfixed. Alaysia picked another shade of blue to add more detail then yellow to add streaks of colour. The image had developed exactly how I thought it might, there in front of me was the abstract angel from the hospital prayer room. Overwhelmed, I stood lost for words. Fang, noticing my inertia, appeared by my side.

"What is it?" she asked.

"You know how you said that you don't like coincidences? Here's another one. The morning after the strike, I visited the prayer room at the hospital. There was a mural of an angel on the back wall, Alaysia's drawing it."

"An angel's a common enough thing to draw, are you sure it's the same one?"

"Yeah, it looked hand painted, a one-off, at least I've never seen the like before or since, until now."

"When you were attached to her, could she have read your mind?"

"I doubt it, anyway, I wasn't even thinking about the angel or the hospital, Alaysia must have been to the prayer room and seen it for herself."

"And you went to the prayer room as well?"

"Yeah, just before I bumped into you, seems like an age ago now."

"Why did you go to the prayer room?" Fang was looking at me with widened eyes and a half smile.

"I thought it would be a good place to seek a bit of solace, the whole out-of-body thing was getting to me and, not that I'm religious, I ended up praying for help but nothing happened..." My sentence had tapered off for it dawned on me in that moment that something had happened, I had just said as much, directly after leaving the prayer room I had met Fang. Was Fang the help that I had so earnestly prayed for? Before I could process my astonishing thought, Alaysia's Grandma walked through to the lounge, cup of tea in hand, and a conversation started. She paid Alaysia a compliment on her drawing before getting to the heart of the matter.

"Are you thinking of your appointment?"

"Yes," answered Alaysia, looking up towards her grandma with a furrowed brow.

"There's nothing to worry about, it won't hurt I'm sure, and I'll be with you."

"Can I blow the candle out again?"

"Yes, of course, and you can have the day off school, as long as you do something school related in the morning." Alaysia's furrows began to dissipate.

"Painting?"

"Yes, that will be fine." And with that, her grandma moved to the settee.

"What did she mean by blow the candle out?" enquired Fang, who I was now looking at in an entirely different light. Though was it just my roller coaster imagination, how could she be the help that I had prayed for, Fang was just as nonplussed with our predicament as I was. After a long pause, spent thinking more about Fang than the candle, I answered the question.

"I'm not sure, there was a candle in the prayer room but it wasn't a real one, they wouldn't allow such a thing in a hospital nowadays, it was an electronic device."

"Those can be blown out too, if it's that type, with a sensor."

"That probably explains it. Perhaps she wants to blow

the candle out to make a wish, that's not unusual. I wonder what she would wish for?"

"The hospital must be investigating her for something, it sounds conclusive she's been there. Maybe, she's just wishing to be better."

"It might be serious," I said with a tinge of dread, fearing that Alaysia might be in danger.

"Not necessarily and, in any case, she seems healthy enough. Let's have another look around and see if we can find anything to do with the hospital."

Doubly determined, but doubly challenged as we now had links between Alaysia and the castle and Alaysia and the hospital to find, we looked around the house once more.

It was not long before the calendar on the corkboard in the kitchen drew Fang's attention. Scribbles against several dates earlier in the month hinted at visits to friends and the return of library books. However, it was an entry for the week ahead that Fang put her finger against. It read CT S 3.30 (fast).

"What do you make of this?" she asked. I considered for a moment.

"Perhaps, CT is the initials of a friend and S means school, they finish at 3.30, at least Lou's does. They are meeting a friend, perhaps going for tea."

"Why write fast in brackets though?"

"I'm not sure, what do you think?"

"Fast could mean not to eat. If CT S stands for CT scan, this would make sense as for these types of tests fasting is sometimes required beforehand. The scan could be at 3.30."

"I think you have it. Fang, the letter rack."

Fang followed me to the letter rack on the window

sill. I pointed out three letters where the top of a pale blue insignia could be seen which I now surmised was that of the NHS. I hadn't thought of the letters in this way when I originally spotted them, and it had taken Fang's latest deduction for me to make the connection. I explained that they could be hospital letters and that it was possible there could be similar ones in the box we saw in the display cabinet. The facts suggested that Alaysia was being investigated for a medical issue, a potentially serious one, and we now had the link to the hospital. Another thought occurred to us; was a medical condition a source of physical trauma and the reason why I could attach to Alaysia? It seemed the strongest of possibilities.

Our search of the house had gone as far as it could, only listening to Alaysia's conversation would provide us with more clues. The situation was tantalising; it felt like we should keep close to Alaysia, after all, I still owed her for saving me, but we had our own business to attend to. The need to bear witness to my body's behaviour with Lou and at work had started to niggle away at me; we decided to take the next opportunity to leave. At least the hospital appointment gave us a rendezvous where we could meet up with Alaysia and we vowed that we would not, under any circumstances, miss it.

CHAPTER TWENTY-TWO

We had left Alaysia in the early afternoon after a neighbour called round. It was too late for a visit to the castle, and, as we were both anxious to see our respective bodies, we had walked to the city centre where Fang could go straight back to the hotel and I could catch a tram home. As we approached the tram stop nearest the hotel, my thoughts turned to domestic matters.

"I really should get the next tram home; I can use this stop," I said, pausing as I considered my next words. Our adventuring had eclipsed my worries but now they had returned and my nerve was beginning to fail me. "I can't deny it will feel odd with you not by my side, really odd."

"You'll miss me?" teased Fang, though there was no denying that's what I meant.

"And who knows what the next twenty-four hours have in store, for both of us?"

"You're worried?"

"Terrified? I feel like my earthly life is about to fall

apart, at home and work."

"I'll come with you if you like." There was nothing else that I would have liked more but I felt I had to refuse.

"No, it's fine, you've got your own worries. But tomorrow, as soon as we can, we should meet up. I've not forgotten about the castle."

"Of course, try to get here, to the hotel, by midday, I'll be waiting." A tram soon appeared and I started my sombre journey. Fang's absence took some getting used to. Having been side by side for five days, and rarely a whisper away from one another, I kept on turning to my right, eager to catch her expression, just to see empty space. Why had I not taken Fang up on her offer to come with me? She had brought unrivalled companionship since we met, dragging me from my solemn shroud into her world of enthusiasm and audacity. With Fang, it felt like I could face the world head-on, without her my inclination was to shy away.

Back at the house, the lights were on but there was no sign of Lou's car. I panicked, why wasn't she here? It was against her Sunday evening routine. Then it struck me. How could I have forgotten? Lou had talked about the school trip to Belgium for months, Lou had volunteered her services and her car would be parked up at school while she was away, from Saturday to next Sunday. And then I felt relief, there was every chance that Lou had left before my body had returned and there would have been no chance for him to cause her any more upset.

Although already dark, the living room curtains were open and within was my body, sat watching television. I counted my blessings, at least he was in one piece, at least he was here and at least Lou was out of harm's way. My body's bedraggled appearance made me question if he would even bother going to work. I walked to the rear and looked through the kitchen window. A takeaway pizza box on the work surface told me of the poor diet my body had adopted. The pizza was from the local takeaway whose relentless advertising, a leaflet through the letterbox every other week, seemed to have paid off and presented another example of how my body had succumbed to the latent power of marketing and suggestion.

I took up position on the garden bench and started to take stock. I did not want to go to work in the morning but I felt a sense of duty, if my body went then I should follow. As the stars gathered in the darkness above, I thought a little deeper about Fang's questions. What was the link between me and the portrait at the gallery? More particularly, what was the link between me and the girl whose portrait it was, the girl in the image of Alaysia? I probed my mind, somewhere within the deep recesses must be the answer but nothing came. What if I looked at things from another angle? There was something else Fang had said, that we had found the portrait because we had followed her body to the gallery. Although, the reality of the situation was that Fang had followed her body and I had followed Fang, already enchanted by her presence.

What was it about Fang? I thought of how she had fluttered around me, always checking my expression and throwing smiles back with the odd look of surprise if I told her an unusual fact. And fluttering was the word for her movements, she was so light on her feet, so deft in her turns that I could believe she had invisible wings to help her along. Wings, I thought, just like the abstract angel. My mind made a sudden and heady association; was it the abstract angel herself that had answered my heartfelt prayer for help and had she manifested herself in Fang's celestial image? Was Fang an angel?

CHAPTER TWENTY-THREE

It was around eight o'clock when my body emerged from the house in my office uniform: light blue shirt, open at the collar, black belted trousers and grey jacket. We were going to work. I had spent the night on the garden bench having dozed off with thoughts that Fang was an angel sweetly circulating my mind. In the cold morning light, I was not so certain about my theory and knowing how easily my mind could run away with itself, I decided not to mention any of it to Fang. I supposed that I could ask Fang directly if she was an angel but even as a spirit it felt too strange a question to ask.

I had moved to the front of the house in anticipation of my body leaving for work and followed him as he set off in the direction of the tram terminus. The walk was brisk and we didn't pass many people, but those we did had consistently given my body a wide birth while staring down at the pavement. These reactions raised my curiosity, and I moved ahead to look back at my body to see a fierce unflinching face with fixed pinpoint pupils.

Little wonder, then, that oncomers were moving over and then avoiding eye contact.

The tram provided a less fretful journey than the previous week's ride in the boot of Lou's car but this only meant I had more capacity to worry about work. We were behind my usual schedule and it was five to nine when we walked through the first-floor office doors, only to be stopped in our tracks. The office looked different, was this even the right floor? Then it struck me, there had been a rearrangement of desks.

Rachel appeared by my body's side.

"There's been an office shuffle while you were out, they've separated us. I'm at the far end and Costa's next to the printing area. You're just here, next to Ida."

"Thanks, Rachel," my body said as he moved to investigate his new station and powered up his laptop. "Why the change?"

"It's Greg's doing, he doesn't feel it appropriate that we should have friends and communicate with each other in the office so he's split certain people up. He sent an email out saying that there's too much talking in the office and we should keep our social lives out of the workplace."

"Jeez, it's like been in the last century," said my body, who looked towards Costa who had come over to join the conversation.

"You mean the century before that, don't you?" interjected Costa. My body nodded his agreement.

"And that's not all," continued Rachel. "Greg went off the scale after you left, sent another email out about a general lack of professionalism in the office, the cheek of the man. We've all got to be in the office by eight thirty at the latest on Mondays from today, no excuses for lack of preparation for the nine o'clock debrief, well, you can imagine."

"It's been horrendous," added Costa.

"Anything else I should know," asked my body. Costa obliged.

"Plenty, Pete's been signed off with stress, I'm hoping it won't be long before Greg moves on. If I know his type, he might be out of here in the new year when he's collected his bonus and before some of the businesses that this place has launched start falling over. I'm telling you now, it'll only take a downturn for things to come to light."

"I wouldn't be too sure he will move on," said Rachel, "Even if there was a downturn he would deflect the blame very nicely, deny all knowledge of what was happening and accuse staff of making up figures. The only manager pushing back is Ada. Oh, there's a rumour she might be moved sideways, not sending the right messages to staff."

"Someone needs to bury him," said Costa looking up at the clock, nine o'clock had arrived

As usual, the Monday morning meeting had come far too quickly, and before my body's laptop had booted up. We filtered into the conference room where Greg was already seated at the head of the table, arms folded across his chest, face set like flint. Instead of starting with the usual updates Greg immediately turned his attention to my body.

"Have they got back to you yet?" he said, referring to the software company that was holding up his prized application. It seemed that the whole room was now staring at my body, their expressions frozen.

"Who's they?"

"Don't get smart with me, you know I mean the software start-up."

"I don't know if they've got back to me. I've not had a chance to catch up, I had most of last week off."

"So what, I'm up to speed and I've had two days off, it's called the weekend." Greg sneered as he turned to his toadies, who broke their expressions to return smirks.

"Fine, I'll go and check now." My body left his chair and moved towards the door.

"Sit down. This explains why I've demanded everyone be in at half past eight, to prepare properly for this meeting."

"Well, have it at ten if you're that bothered, or, even better, have it Friday. Anyway, you asked a question, I hate to be unprofessional so I'll go and get an answer for you."

"Sit down," repeated Greg, this time barking the words out. My body ignored his instruction and walked calmly from the conference room and back to his desk. With the laptop now booted up, he searched his emails to find that the company had still not replied. He turned to go back into the conference room but found Greg blocking his way. "They've not got back; I think it's about time to scrap you're not so star project."

"Never."

Greg took a step forward and his reddened face was within a foot of my body. Greg was about to let rip when my body shoved him hard against the shoulder.

"Get out of my personal space you jerk." Greg stumbled but came back again.

"Do that again."

My body obliged, only this time he shoved harder.

Greg tripped over a briefcase which had been left by the side of the adjacent desk and found himself sprawled on the floor, staring up with eyes blazing. My body was looking far from apologetic, his right leg moved back as if preparing to kick Greg. I looked away.

"Any more requests, you crook?"

"Get out of here, now," Greg yelled.

"Fine, bye." My body turned to his desk, thankfully having not kicked Greg, shut the laptop lid and walked out of the office.

"And don't come back."

I followed my body to the building entrance but hung back, he looked unbothered by the fracas while I was filled with alarm. What would be said about my future upstairs? I decided that I should go back and listen to the aftermath. As I stood, and as my body walked out, Fang walked in.

"Fang, am I glad to see you," I said, relief etched on my face.

"What's happened?" asked my friend as she stared back at my body who was striding off in the direction of the tram stop.

"The mother of all arguments," I responded then described the clash with Greg in detail. At the end of my narrative, Fang's eyes lit up.

"Is he really a crook?"

"I think he's up to something, having said that he's too clever to get caught at whatever it is. The rumour is that his bonus depends on the number of successful grant applications and that's what drives his sick behaviour but it can't be just that. There must be another reason for his madness or, perhaps, that's it, he's mad, a sociopath."

"Where's he now?"

"Still in the morning meeting, probably."

"Where's his computer?"

"He has a laptop which will be on his desk, one of his toadies runs the meeting from their laptop."

"Does his laptop have a touch screen?" I realised where Fang was heading.

"I think it does."

We were soon on the third floor and with only a couple of other people around were free to use Greg's laptop. We tapped the screen and found ourselves staring at his desktop.

"IT policy," beamed Fang, "always lock your computer when not at your desk. When will they learn?"

As my finger followed Fang's, a list of the most recently viewed files appeared on the screen. Working our way down the list, all looked routine until we opened a spreadsheet that showed the annual accounts of a marketing company which were marked as confidential.

"He shouldn't have those," I said, "they're the accounts of the marketing company we recommend with virtually every grant application nowadays. The project I'm on with at the moment has thousands of pounds worth of work with them."

"You said he shouldn't have their accounts?"

"That's right, he shouldn't have anything to do with a company we recommend, if he did then he'd have to declare an interest in the application, which he never has." We navigated to the marketing company's web page to find their CEO. Then we checked Greg's messaging accounts for the corresponding name and a string of messages appeared. It became clear that Greg would benefit greatly from the CEO if we secured work with his company.

"What do you make of these?" asked Fang.

"He's taking backhanders, it's fraud. We had thirty successful applications in the last year and virtually all secured contracts for this marketing company. Even if the start-up business fails within the first few years, the marketing will have been discharged and profits made. Greg must be making thousands."

Just then Greg walked into the office with one of his toadies, Colin.

"We have to work quickly, who should we send these files and messages to, so he gets the justice he deserves," said Fang. From my conversation with the auditor, I knew exactly where to send the information.

"Alison from the Local Development Office and I can remember her email address. But we haven't the time, he's right here." Greg was standing some six feet away and had started a conversation with Colin.

"He'll never work here again," said Greg. It was obvious he was talking about me and, with the few people in the office out of earshot, Greg started waxing lyrical about how it was good management practice to get rid of people.

"Chop, chop," said Fang grabbing my attention back. "Let's get this done, follow my finger."

Within a minute, we had sent an email with the incriminating evidence attached; Greg's position was now in danger. We listened as he finished his conversation.

"...usual place for lunch Col? Great stuff. I best get on, by the end of the morning, Fred will be off the books. I'll stop his pay from last Monday, every penny counts." Greg rubbed his thumb against his forefinger, he was in full gloating mode as people so often are just before their downfall.

So, I was to come off the books. I was not too concerned as once Greg's misdemeanours came to light then there was every chance that I'd be asked back and, in any case, my morning's adventure had helped me decide that my future lay elsewhere, a space where I could use my imagination and stay in Nottingham. What I was concerned about, however, was that my body had nearly used violence. It might only take a wrong word by someone and he could flip; I feared his further adventures may end up in a police cell.

"I'd like to stick around to see his face when he gets an email back from the Local Development Office," I said, "but my body's getting worse, more aggressive. The look on his face when Greg was on the floor, I thought he was going in for the kill. If I don't get back into my body soon who knows what I'll be going back to; we need to find answers."

"That's the reason I came to fetch you. I've some news," said Fang.

"News?"

"This morning, my body delivered her presentation on her first week in the UK."

"How did it go?"

"There were a lot of photos."

"Makes sense, she'd taken a lot."

"The thing is, I started to notice something."

"Fang, what is it?"

"There were fewer people in the images than I remember when she took them." I stared directly into Fang's eyes. Her short sentence sent shivers through me as I started to anticipate where the conversation was leading. “Remember the castle entrance?”

“Of course.”

“Remember that couple, he had a red suit, she had a blue dress?”

“Yeah.”

“Remember the children running round them?”

“Yeah.”

“They weren’t in the image; it was the couple alone.”

I had no doubt what my friend had said was true but was there another explanation, I already knew there would not be, I asked anyway.

“Could she have taken another photo, when the children had scooted?”

“No, I’m certain. She only took that one and moved on, I remember because, at the time, I thought she was taking the photo because of the children. And, it was definitely that Saturday, she had dated the image.”

The implication was clear enough.

“The children – they were spirits.”

CHAPTER TWENTY-FOUR

The onset of rain ensured that the castle grounds were quiet though there was a healthy enough queue at the museum entrance. The revelation that Fang and I had walked past spirits in this very place meant that we had set off from my office without delay and with unguarded enthusiasm. Our first destination was to be the gallery, but as we walked through the museum, my enthusiasm turned to nervousness. What would be awaiting us? We turned into the long room and headed straight for the portrait section to see, as we remembered them, the collection of paintings of children. At the centre was the portrait that, to my memory, had so looked like Alaysia, now there was little doubt about the likeness.

"Astonishing," said Fang, "it's Alaysia, at least it looks exactly like her."

Our eyes moved to the notice in front of us which gave several paragraphs of information about the display of portraits. We stood and silently read. I was barely halfway through the first paragraph before my heart was aching and I understood that the value of these small portraits to some would outweigh that of a grandmaster. The notice explained that in the early nineteenth century child mortality rates were atrocious with more than a fifth of children dying before the age of ten, victims of diseases, poverty and child labour. In an age where there were no photographs then a portrait was a way for a grieving family to preserve the image of their child for remembrance and the display was a collection of posthumous portraits, painted shortly after the children had died. Their small size signified the limited time and budget that would often be available, even the examples shown were far beyond the means of most families and such a portrait was considered a luxury. A luxury? - I could barely read on for sorrow. A note relating to Alaysia's image explained that the artist and the subject were not known though flowers in a portrait signified that the parents hoped their children would be reborn in better times; in the portrait, the girl clutched a red rose.

I thought of how the girl in Alaysia's likeness might have died and how devastated her parents must have been, my sorrow deepened. I did not have to look at Fang, who stood uncharacteristically silent, to understand she was feeling similarly. After half a minute or so, she broke the silence.

"So sad, isn't it?" Overwhelmed with grief, I could not answer. I sensed Fang turning towards me. "Are you okay?" I steeled myself, trying to summon up a sentence I might finish.

"I wish we knew more," I stuttered, "about the portrait I mean, but even if we did, it wouldn't help. We can't change the past."

Nothing could have prepared me for what happened

next.

"...but you can shape the future," said a small voice that came from behind us. We turned in unison and, although dressed differently in a charcoal grey dress, there was little doubt that standing before us was the girl in the portrait. I looked down to the floor, none of us were casting shadows from the gallery lighting. I felt enchanted by our spirit companion and my newly awakened sorrow lightened, but words were not forthcoming.

"Hi I'm Fang, and this is..." My friend prompted me and in doing so rescued me from my silence. I felt my expression softening.

"I'm Fred, plain old Fred."

"And I'm plain old Eliza," said the girl, whose earnest stare had turned to a smile.

"It's great to see you, Eliza," said Fang, "you're the girl in the portrait, with the yellow dress and rose?"

"That's me."

"You died and you're a spirit?"

"That's right. How did you die?" Eliza had got straight to the crux of the matter and as I stalled in surprise, Fang obliged with an answer.

"We didn't die, we were struck by lightning and were thrown out of our bodies. We think we're spirits though, like you. Our bodies are still alive and we have been trying to re-join them."

Eliza considered Fang's words.

"In a kind of way, that's what I'm trying to do, you see after I died, my ma promised I would be reborn, and I've been waiting for a long time. I heard you talking, the girl you said looks exactly like me, Alaysia, she could be who I'm meant to be. If I meet her, I'll know."

"Who you're meant to be?" queried Fang.

"My match, the person I can join."

"Eliza, I'm sure we can help. To start with, why don't you tell us your story?"

The conversation had already taken an intriguing turn and my mind was in overdrive. Fang, on the other hand, seemed measured and guided Eliza and me to the bench in the centre of the gallery to avoid the disruption of the occasional visitor walking the line of paintings. Fang and I sat on either side of Eliza, me with a burning curiosity. Eliza braced herself as if telling her story would bring back the trauma, I braced myself too, and with a solemn expression, she began her tale.

"I died working in a cotton mill, it was my first day working there."

"Oh, Eliza..." I said, the words coming out spontaneously as if I was living the raw pain of heartache, and then a griever's silence overcame me, I could say no more. I was heartbroken.

"It's okay," said Eliza, "The year was 1822, I had just turned nine and had an older sister and two older brothers. We lived with our parents in two rooms of a cold, dark, damp terrace house. We had little money for food so I followed my ma and sister into the cotton mill. My ma had promised us fresh bread at the end of the day, she said there was nothing like the smell of fresh bread. It was a cold January day and we dressed in the dark and made our way to the mill, the thought of the bread keeping me going. As soon as we arrived, I was put to work underneath the weaving machinery to collect the threads that could be used again. The noise was deafening, it was cold and the work terrifying, worse than I had imagined. The belts and wheels whirled round at speed in the space where I had to crawl.

"At least my ma worked in the same room as I did and could keep half an eye on me, though I could see she was as scared as I was. The day was long, and all I had to show for my work was thirst and hunger; I hated that this was to be my life. By our third break, late in the afternoon, I was longing for the fresh bread. I could hardly stay awake but there was one last shift to do. I can't remember what happened with the confusion caused by my tiredness and fright. I might have fainted, but whatever it was, I got caught in the machinery. I felt a pulling at my arm and was dragged along the floor. I heard tearing and then my ma's scream. The next thing, I'm picking myself up from the wall next to the large windows, and I thought I had been thrown clear.

"They stopped the machine and I could hear my ma's cries. I called her but she didn't turn, no one turned. A woman scurried under the machine and shouted for help, several others rushed over and joined her. I got up and walked over to my ma and found myself dazed but otherwise unhurt. I touched my ma's arm but such was her distress, or so I thought, she didn't feel it. I felt numb when I realised what was happening, another child had been injured, caught in the belt. They carried her out and to my horror the child was me. My ma held my body and begged me not to leave her. The others shook their heads, my body had died. But who or what was I? No one could see me, no one could hear me and no one could feel my touch. It was terrible to see my ma's sadness, she stayed with my body and I stayed with her.

"Not long after, the machine was restarted and everyone got back to work as if nothing had happened. My ma was allowed to leave, with my older sister, to take my body home and carried me towards the gates of a mill along the road. As we got near, the workers began to leave and I realised this was where my pa worked. A neighbour rushed over and burst into tears, grabbing onto my ma when she saw what had happened, the two of them holding each other up. As the street busied with people crisscrossing in their rush home from the many mills, I caught sight of my pa in the crowd as he talked with two other men. My neighbour called him and he looked up in surprise, his face whitened when he realised what must've happened. He ran over and fell to his knees. My ma leaned into him and they held my body between them, both sobbing. Rain was falling, I couldn't feel it, I wasn't feeling cold, I was a spirit. When my family left for home, I followed them. What else could I do?"

Eliza's question did not need to be answered and we all paused for a moment. Eliza's story had touched me deeply and with the candour with which she had spoken then I no longer felt like a stranger. Fang raised her forefingers to her lips with her hands clasped beneath, as if in prayer.

"Eliza, the portrait, how did it come about?" she asked. Eliza braced herself once more and then continued her story.

"When they got my body home, talk turned to a burial. My pa repeated over and over that he could not bear the thought of never seeing my face again, fearing that he would forget what I looked like. It was one of my aunties who suggested the portrait, she knew of a local family who had their son painted after he had died of cholera, so they could remember him. The artist was a student of art and she had insisted on not taking a fee.

My parents agreed and my aunty set off to find her. After sitting my body up on the bed, my ma busied herself tidying her hair, she brushed it through continuously, speaking to me all the time. Any strands of hair that caught on the brush were carefully set aside as a keepsake. My aunty returned with the artist who said it was her privilege to help. My favourite colour is yellow so she painted me in a yellow dress. My ma kept talking to me, tears flowing all the while, telling me how this wasn't the end, how I would be reborn in better times and how she was sure that, with God's grace, we'd find each other. It was the artist that suggested the red rose, a symbol of rebirth."

I had listened intently as Eliza had spoken, everything she had said resonated deep within me. It was as if I had been expecting some of the details and, as Fang's observations were about to demonstrate, perhaps not surprisingly so.

"Eliza, which arm got caught?" asked Fang.

"Here," responded Eliza, pointing to her right arm just above the elbow. "Why do you ask?"

"Alaysia had a long birthmark at that exact point. Fred, do you remember?" I nodded my agreement. "And Alaysia's painting of the mournful scene outside the mill, as if she was aware of the moment Eliza's father heard the dreadful news of his daughter's death. Fred, do you see? The link between the portrait and Alaysia, it's far beyond the physical likeness. Eliza and Alaysia share the same history, they were separated by death two centuries ago. It's time for them to be reunited, we must help."

I understood Eliza's interest, Alaysia was her destiny, promised by her mother, and a permanent residence where, if the match worked, she could come alive and flourish. And I understood Fang's enthusiasm but, in my mind, a dilemma had formed. Was helping the right thing to do? What about Alaysia's wishes? But was there any doubt about this match? The likeness between the two girls, Alaysia's visions of the sorrowful scene outside the mill and her marked arm, were these signs of reincarnation, of rebirth and would spirit attachment complete the arc? Or was something more sinister lurking? In helping would we be committing some act of sacrilege that would go against the rules of the supernatural world? Then again, what rules? And, if the match worked then wouldn't this be proof enough that it was destined? My mind was circling, I could not decide if helping was the right thing to do or not. There was but one thing to do, give the decision over to my heart. I could not stand the thought of Eliza's dimpled smile turning to hollow cheeks of despair, I could not be part of that, the answer was yes – I would help.

CHAPTER TWENTY-FIVE

As Fang's assertion that Alaysia was Eliza's destiny settled upon me, it was as if I was seeing a glimmer of light into another world. I had always thought of reincarnation, memories of previous lives and spirits to be disparate things of romance until ten days ago. Now, I was believing them all and seeing they were related. And we had the link between Alaysia and the portrait. Not just the similarity of physical features but, somehow, Alaysia seemed to have an inherited memory of Eliza's life and a physical remnant of her trauma. Were Alaysia and Eliza really one and the same? Would their union complete the spiritual arc? Furthermore, Fang and I had found both Alaysia and Eliza, we had discovered their connection and now had the opportunity to help them match - was this the reason we had been jettisoned into the spirit world?

Fang's observations were not lost on Eliza.

"Doesn't what you've said show Alaysia has got to be my match," she said. "If only I could meet her. Where does Alaysia live?" Eliza turned from Fang to me with nervous, piercing eyes as if there was a dependency hanging on the answer.

"A house in Castle Meadow, between here and the river," I answered.

"Oh," said Eliza, as if the obstacle she was anticipating had been realised.

"Is there a problem?"

"Have you been to Alaysia's house?"

"Yeah, she lives with her grandma, we were there just two days ago."

"Then you can travel further than I can."

"What do you mean?"

"I can't go further than the rock."

"The rock?"

"Let me show you." And with that Eliza stood up and headed to the gallery exit, turning back to us as she did so. "Come on, we're going to the café, the place always makes me feel brighter and there is a fine view from there." We headed out of the gallery, through the small rooms of the museum, through the gift shop and found ourselves in the café standing by the very window where Fang and I had sat on our first day together. As the smattering of customers sat unknowingly, Eliza looked out onto the terrace and pointed through the glass panelling to the tip of the rock outcrop that dropped over a hundred feet below us.

"Look, the rock, the foundation on which old Nottingham is built upon. The rock ends there and that's as far south as I can go. Castle Meadow is down there, isn't it?" Eliza pointed in the general direction of the estate.

"That's right," answered Fang with beaming eyes. "I

presume you can go as far as the hospital, to the west?"

"Yes, the hospital was built on the site where the cotton mill used to be, that's about the furthest west I can go."

"Fred, do you remember, there was an outcrop just beyond the hospital, that must mark the western boundary of the rock." I realised what Eliza was telling us, her movements were confined by the bedrock beneath our feet and my curiosity mounted.

"But why can't you go outside the rock?" I asked.

"If I try then everything darkens," replied Alaysia, "it's as if I am becoming enveloped in a mist and who knows what lurks beyond it, whatever it is, I'm not ready for it. I have to stay within the area of the rock."

"Eliza, we can help you," said Fang, "Alaysia is visiting the hospital on Wednesday afternoon; we can take you to meet her."

"Brilliant." Eliza's eyes widened. "And will you stay with me until then, both of you?"

"If you like," said Fang looking across at me.

"For sure," I responded. I had no wish to leave and was eager to learn more about our new acquaintance. Fang's curiosity also showed no sign of abating.

"How far does the rock run to the East?" she asked.

"To the far side of the shopping centre where there's an entrance to the network of caves that run underground to the castle, they are a tourist attraction nowadays."

"And to the North."

"There's a theatre at the top of the city, that's about the limit."

Essential as Fang's enquiries undoubtedly were, I had only half listened to the conversation as a question had started to burn inside of me. Despite Eliza's ability to roam across the city, we had found her right beside the object that seemed to be the spiritual centre of all our adventures.

"Eliza, your portrait, it's the most beautiful painting, how did it come to the museum?" I asked.

"It's a long story," replied Eliza.

"Do tell us Eliza, and why don't we take a seat?" And we took up position at the table by the window as Eliza began her narrative.

"After my body was buried, I thought I would end up in heaven, but nothing changed. So, I stayed by my ma's side, day after day, night after night, watching and waiting. My pa changed, he hardly spoke after my death and he never forgave himself for not being able to provide for us all, that's why I ended up at the mill.

"My family cherished my portrait and saved up to buy the frame that is with the painting to this day. I saw my brothers grow up and leave. Both my ma and pa died in their sleep of conditions I couldn't tell you the names of. My portrait passed to my sister who had married and lived nearer the castle, which was still in ruin after being destroyed in riots. I decided to stay with my portrait and my sister. She had five children and, eventually, the portrait was passed to the eldest daughter who also lived within the rock. She was a dressmaker who never married and when she died her house was cleared, which helped pay for her funeral. There were few items of value, just my portrait and some precious items of jewellery, at least they had been precious to my ma. The jewellery was bought by a local trader and my portrait was donated to the castle, which by now had been restored and turned into a museum. With no relations, that I knew of, living on the rock, I stayed with my portrait and the castle became my home. The portrait wasn't displayed at first, it was held in a storeroom and time seemed to stand still. However, that changed when my portrait was taken from storage, cleaned and displayed alongside several similar paintings, we had our own section in the gallery. It was like a new beginning, for all of us."

The conclusion of Eliza's narrative had made Fang and I sit upright.

Us. I remembered why we had rushed to the gallery, the missing children from the photo taken at the castle entrance. Fang was also making the connection.

"Eliza, the other children's portraits, they have spirits too?" she asked.

"Some of them, they're my friends. I think you've seen them already," said Eliza.

"The costume day, the other Saturday, you were there with your friends?"

"That's right. Normally, we avoid big crowds but everyone loves the costume day, it's as if our pasts have come to life again, it's always so exciting."

"And you were all dancing round the woman with the huge blue dress in the tunnel at the castle entrance?"

"Right again, I knew you'd seen us." I was taken aback, despite our best efforts, Fang and I had walked past, even nearly collided with, spirits on our first day and had not been aware of it; how many others had we unknowingly seen during our adventures?

"We noticed you," Eliza continued, "when Carla rushed by, you both moved to get out of her way, obviously you had seen her. When you stepped out of the tunnel into the daylight, we could see that you and

Fred did not cast even the slightest bit of a shadow and we knew you were spirits. Your lookalike, Fang, was clearly a living soul and we thought you were trying to match with her."

"Match?"

"Yes, to join together with her"

"That's exactly what I was trying to do, we've been calling it re-attach. But why not speak to us?"

"We're wary of new spirits and keep our distance, at least until we know their intentions, not all spirits are friendly."

I understood Eliza and her friend's reluctance, I had been instinctively wary of other spirits until I had met Fang, since which times I had grown in confidence, now a twinge of fear had returned. Had dangers been lurking? I was beginning to feel foolhardy, after all, Fang and I had casually sought out spirits and their hauntings, yet no harm had befallen us. Had we been afforded some level of protection? With those thoughts, another question was thrown to the forefront of my mind; were Fang and I being guided along on our strange adventure?

CHAPTER TWENTY-SIX

"Eliza," said Fang "If we take you to Alaysia, could you attach to her?"

"I hope so, I know it's possible. But spirits can only attach to people who let them in and, even then, only in certain places. Some of my friends have found their match."

"Their matches? Tell us about them."

Fang and I settled back as Eliza took us back in time once more.

"Aaron was the last spirit to match at the castle. He had been killed in the castle riots that destroyed the original building and came to us after a huge etching of the riots took centre stage in the history section of the museum. Aaron is in the etching with another boy, both looking on at the burning castle.

"It is the belief passed down by spirits that we will all find our place, it is only a matter of time, and Aaron's time came in the summer around thirty years ago. Aaron, me and a few others were in the castle grounds when Jasmine, another friend, found us. She had seen a boy in the military section of the museum who looked exactly like Aaron. By the time we found the lookalike he was in the gift shop. What Jasmine had said was true, the boy had Aaron's face. Aaron was convinced he had found his destiny, he said goodbye to us and walked into the boy, but just bounced back."

"We know how that feels," I interjected. Eliza continued.

"Although disappointed, Aaron was convinced that this was his time to join the human race again so we followed the boy into the café. He stood in the queue at the counter and Aaron tried once more, it worked and Aaron and the boy became one. They looked fine, better than fine; the boy's mood improved and he started talking about the history of the castle."

"Could Aaron see you, once he'd attached?"

"I don't think so, it was as if we were not there, though we were sure that Aaron was okay. You see, Aaron used to wink occasionally when he told you something and the boy started doing just this. The boy would return now and again to the museum, spending a lot of time in the history section, it was probably Aaron's influence, the etching of the riots is still on show today."

"You said some of your friends, there's been other matches?"

"Two others, another in the café and one on the terrace just outside. We think that there's something special about the area around the café. It might have been where the chapel of the old castle was or something like that."

Fang sat back and sighed.

"To think that on that first day, there was an

opportunity for me to re-attach. If only we had known that there is something about the café."

As the news of the attachments, in the very room where we sat, settled upon me, I suddenly remembered my own experience.

"Eliza, I should have told you earlier, but I've only just thought about it. I was briefly attached to Alaysia, in a cavern at Matlock Bath." I told Eliza of the whole episode: about the affinity I had felt for Alaysia in the amusement arcade, about the darkness that surrounded me as we descended into the hillside and about my salvation at the hands of the very person we had chosen to follow. Finally, I told of how the likeness between Alaysia and the portrait had prompted our return to the gallery. Eliza had looked on with the faintest of smiles as I concluded my story. Fang's reaction was somewhat different, she straightened up with her index fingers touching her lips.

"Eliza," said Fang, "do you know of other places that are good for matching, anywhere in the hospital?"

"I don't know of any in the hospital," replied Eliza, "but I do know of one at the far end of the shopping centre, by the entrance to the network of caves I told you about, right next to an antiques shop."

"All Things Past and Present?"

"You know it?"

"We followed my body there. To think, I missed two places where I might have re-attached." Fang crossed her eyebrows. "You know what, I remember the waiter here recommended that shop, another coincidence." Eliza's eyes widened. "Eliza?"

"I think it's time we went to the forest, I'll introduce you to the others. Come on."

We headed back into the body of the museum and down a set of stairs, a sign overhead proclaimed 'The Hood Forest - an exhibition on the times of Robin of Sherwood.' As we descended, I felt a growing sense of anticipation, more spirits awaited us. At the bottom of the stairs, we found ourselves staring in surprise at what we saw before us. Gone were the polished floors, formal walkways and glass cabinets of the museum. Here was a large room with cloth ribbons in many shades of green, red and yellow draped from a low-hanging ceiling – *a place of fun*.

We followed Eliza along a woodland path painted on the floor. Tree trunks, which stretched to the ceiling, lined the way together with the occasional interactive display board showing forest flora and fauna. Sporadically, beams of light shone from on high, simulating sunlight permeating through a leafy canopy, it was as if walking through a forest. We made our way to the back wall where a large screen was showing a film on wildlife. In front, was a huge comfy sofa draped in patchwork throws of rustic green, red and brown, and on either side of the sofa were two comfy armchairs similarly decorated. Three small figures were sunk deep into the sofa cushioning, and Eliza stopped right behind the trio.

"I'd like to introduce you to my friends," she announced. Her friends turned around in surprise as Eliza continued, pointing to each of them in turn. "This is Jasmine, this is Annabella and this is Clara. Guys, this is Fang and Fred, remember from last Saturday?"

Eliza beamed with pride and the three spirits looked suitably impressed though it was Jasmine who looked particularly interested. She stood up, threw her long dark hair back and circled Fang and I. Jasmine was taller than the other three and, with light blue flared trousers and a dark blue woollen tank top, was unquestionably from more modern times. Annabella and Clara had plain Victorian dresses, and I had no doubt were the contingent, along with Eliza, that had spun around the teddy girl's dress.

"Fang, you're still a spirit," observed Jasmine.

"Sure, look no shadow," replied Fang as she placed her foot under the nearest beam of light.

Eliza anticipated Jasmine's next question and told the others how Fang and I had been struck from our bodies, which were still living. As her audience looked at Fang and me in awe, Eliza told them how our quest to rejoin our bodies had led us to Alaysia who had rescued me from the darkness. Then Eliza shared the news that Alaysia could be her destined match and of the planned rendezvous at the hospital. Jasmine looked pleased for her friend.

"This is great," she said, "of course, I'll come with you, to the hospital, I might be able to help."

"Speaking of help," said Eliza, staring hard at Jasmine. "I've told them of where matches have taken place: in the café and All Things Past and Present," Eliza had emphasised the last part of her sentence. Jasmine took the hint and turned to Fang.

"Ah, you found the place. Did your body get a memento?"

I checked myself for a moment, there was no one in earshot when Fang's body spoke to the waiter so how did Jasmine know about the memento? I looked across at Fang whose scrunched lips expression was aimed at Jasmine.

"Shall we take a seat," said Fang, "I'd love to hear your story and how you attach yourself to the waiter."

Jasmine told her story, how she had died at the hospital after a car crash over fifty years ago. She had been travelling from Wolverhampton on the motorway with her father driving when the accident happened. Having been rushed to hospital she passed away in the emergency room. After leaving her body she was found by a spirit nurse who guided her to the castle where she stayed with the others. About three years ago the waiter started his job in the café and Jasmine found she had an empathy with him. He was gregarious and his conversations with customers were entertaining, for this reason, she started to visit the café more often. She found she could attach to him by accident, at least she thought it was an accident. One morning the waiter had been serving a customer and entered into one of his usual conversations. Jasmine, Eliza and Clara were listening in though it was Jasmine that was closest as they huddled around. Without warning, he side-stepped into Jasmine. Instead of merely bouncing off, which happened with all other accidental collisions, she and the waiter merged; it had been as if they were drawn together like attracting magnets. Jasmine found herself attached and described the thrill to sense breathing and feel a long-forgotten warmth. It was not long, however, before panic set in as Jasmine realised that she could no longer see her spirit companions and in that moment of strong emotion had found herself released and standing by her friends again, who had not moved from the waiter's side during the brief encounter. The next day, and after the scare had subsided, she tried to match, this time deliberately, and it worked. After that, she found she could match and leave at will. The idea of trying to influence the waiter came to mind when she realised the thoughts that she was having when she was attached somehow manifested themselves through his actions. If she thought of how delicious the chocolate cake looked then before long the waiter was recommending it to the customers or eating a piece himself. She found that she could read his thoughts, almost interrupt them, and suggest ideas of her own, ideas such as recommending All Things Past and Present.

"But why All Things Past and Present," I asked.

"The shop has a long history and has collected hundreds of antiquities from the local area. Over the years spirits have made their way there with old cherished items, things like photographs, paintings or jewellery. They use the shop as a base like we use this place as ours. The difference is that we get a lot more visitors, thousands of every week, who we can take a look at, for potential matches. I influenced the waiter to recommend All Things Past and Present so they get more visitors, the spirits there are very appreciative.

"And the good thing about people who come to the museum is that they are drawn to the past, it is not only spirits who are trying to find their match. In the gallery, most visitors pass by the paintings, taking a casual look, even stopping sometimes to read a caption. But occasionally, just occasionally, someone stops at a particular painting, their eyes scanning over the detail. They don't even know why themselves but they feel something, an attraction. It is these people, the people who feel the past, that a spirit might be able to join."

"Have you discovered why you can match with the waiter?" enquired Fang.

"No, but the only place I know where I can match with him is the café, which isn't a problem as that's where he works."

"You must have thought about why you can match with the waiter?"

"Oh, I've thought about it, but nothing has ever stacked up. It's also a puzzle why I can join and leave at will, those that attach to their likeness stay attached. I wondered if the waiter and I were related in some way, and that that was the reason, but I've never recognised any names of contacts I've seen on his phone. I even travelled home with him a few times when I was attached, that was scary, being outside the rock. The odd thing was that his flat was decorated in a way which suited me, I guess you could say we have the same tastes, some like-mindedness, an affinity."

Affinity - the very word I used to describe my draw to Alaysia. The question remained for me, and for Jasmine, why do we feel an affinity?

CHAPTER TWENTY-SEVEN

Eliza, Jasmine, Annabella and Clara had called themselves the spirithood after the place in which they had made their base. As the afternoon wore on, we heard more stories of their earthy lives and the spirit inhabitants of Nottingham.

We learnt of a spirit station master that parades the shopping centre concourse where his station platform used to be and, pocket watch in hand, greets shoppers as they emerge from the many stores as if they were alighting passengers. And of the nurse whose former hospital was now a pub and who had made the modern hospital her home, ready to give a helping hand to new spirits or watch over her modern-day colleagues – a tale that had escaped into local lore. The barman who calls time every night, an aspiring actress who appears on stage and a condemned criminal in the old courtrooms. I asked about the spirits of Queen Isabella and Mortimer to hear that if they had existed then they must have long departed old Nottingham, final destination unknown.

Visitors had come and gone throughout the afternoon but it was only when two school children stopped to play with the interactive display by the side of us that Fang became distracted.

"Can you affect the human world in any way?" she asked, looking from one to the other of the spirithood. I initially thought Fang's interest related just to the workings of the touch screen but there was something else.

Jasmine crossed her eyebrows.

"Why do you ask?"

"The spirit nurse, Fred had heard of the story. If spirits can't interact with the living, how did the living know about the nurse."

Fang's point was an incisive one which had not occurred to me.

"There are other spirits that can attach, fleeting attachments, like me with the waiter, like Fred with Alaysia. Such interactions might leave a trace and emerge through a daydream. It would only take the host to describe what they had envisioned and the tale would be released and spread, such is the thirst for ghost stories."

"Have you ever met spirits like us before,"

"No, never."

"What are you thinking Fang?" I interjected.

"Consider," Fang replied, "you've heard many stories today, when you're back in your body, you might share what you've heard."

The spirithood looked apprehensive.

"You know what," I said in all sincerity, "what is said in the forest, stays in the forest."

And so, we heard many more tales from the

spirithood that afternoon. So absorbed had I been that it was only when the lights dimmed and the power to the screens cut that it occurred to me that the museum had closed, we were locked in. It was not long before Eliza, Annabella and Clara started to doze. Jasmine, however, remained talkative.

"What's happening," asked Fang.

"Oh, they're falling asleep that's all, it's usual after the museum closes," replied Jasmine, "but they're not quite asleep yet. Normally, at this time of evening, I tell them things, things that I've done during the day. If I've ventured out of the castle then I'll describe what I've seen, with a little elaboration, and make up a story. Eliza loves me doing this, it reminds her of her ma who use to invent stories to tell her at bedtime."

"When do you sleep?"

"I feel tired too but it takes a while longer so I sit here with them until I doze off too. How about you two."

"We fall asleep when our bodies do so it varies, normally before midnight."

As Fang and Jasmine chatted quietly away, I fell into the background, lost in my thoughts. Throughout the afternoon a world of spirits had been revealed to us yet it felt that we still had much to discover. I could not shake off the feeling that we were been guided through the vastness of it all, being shown the parts of the spirit world that we needed to see. We had found our way to the gallery where we saw Eliza's portrait and then to Matlock Bath where we met Alaysia. When Eliza revealed herself, we learned of the link between her and Alaysia. Now, we had an opportunity to help them match. Would this really complete a spiritual arc? And was this the purpose of our excursion from humanity?

But why me and Fang?

Sensing Fang standing by me, I was stirred from my thoughts and looked up to see she had her index finger placed across her pursed lips. My eyes turned to the sofa. Jasmine's eyes were closed. Eliza, next to her, looked so peaceful in sleep, the dimples of her smile showing as she slept. Fang beckoned me to follow her and we soon back at our usual table in the café, looking out onto Castle Meadow, the terrace floodlit by the castle lights. I had lots of questions for Fang yet a seemingly innocuous one was at the forefront of my mind.

I wonder why they fall asleep so early," I said. "Do you think it's because they are children and that's what time they would have slept when they were alive?"

"I don't think that's it," replied Fang.

"You have an explanation?"

"Not a very well-formed one, I shouldn't talk of it."

"Try me."

"Okay, what are you thinking about right now?"

"Nothing." Fang looked at me with eyes dipped, her try-harder expression.

"Let me rephrase, who are you thinking about right now or at least several moments ago when you asked why they fall asleep so early?"

"Eliza and her friends."

"Right, concentrate on Eliza for a moment. What if when she died, she was somehow able to tap into people's minds, like we tap into our own body's minds? Maybe, as long as someone is thinking about her, then even without Eliza knowing, she can use that energy. Her mother, father and siblings would think constantly of her after she passed."

"But surely as her family got older, they would think about her less and less."

"Don't underestimate the power of grief, I suspect there would not be a day when they didn't think of her, especially with the portrait."

I began to see very dimly where Fang was heading.

"But when her family had all died, who would think of her then?"

"As the portrait was passed down to her niece, and the story with it, then she would think of Eliza."

"And when the niece died?"

"The portrait came here, and remember Eliza saying that when her portrait was displayed that it was like a new beginning. In the gallery, the visitors would think of Eliza when they saw her portrait and the power of their thoughts would bring her to life. After the visitors leave then their thoughts from the gallery would linger but gently fade away to the back of their minds. As those thoughts fade then Eliza begins to doze."

As not very well-formed theories go, Fang's was, as I expected, a compelling one but just as I was about to sit back in satisfaction, my heart dropped.

"Hang on, Eliza, Carla and Annabella, they have portraits but what about Jasmine? Won't there be a time when Jasmine is out of living memory and she will fade away? It's almost fifty years since her accident, she can't have much time left."

"Jasmine comes from an age of photographs; I think it likely her parents would have a school portrait or holiday snap that they would frame and treasure. And they would, of course, have kept some of her possessions which they would cherish and eventually pass down to later generations. In these ways, they would keep her memory and spirit alive. Or maybe Jasmine's affinity with the waiter may sustain her, it might be that he has some connection with her, in any case, once Jasmine has melded with his mind perhaps there is a part of his memory that is always hers, maybe Jasmine's destiny lies in this direction."

"As long as someone, somehow thinks of them then their spirits can live on."

"Precisely, they live on."

CHAPTER TWENTY-EIGHT

"The most important thing," said Fang, "is we get Eliza and Alaysia matched. We can only hope that somewhere along Alaysia's route through the hospital is a spot where matching is possible. The place is built on the westerly outcrop of the rock so there is at least a chance."

We had awoken in the café in the seats we had taken the night before, and I was still a little in awe at Fang's ability to unravel the inner workings of the spirit world. My lack of aptitude, however, had not stopped my intense curiosity about the mysterious world we inhabited.

"Why is it that only certain places are good for attaching," I asked, "and what has the westerly outcrop got to do with it?" Fang's lips tightened. "Fang, you have a theory?"

"Not a very well-formed one."

"I know, and you shouldn't talk of it, but try me."

"Think about the places where attachments have

happened. Here in the cafe, we are at the tip of the rock on which Nottingham is built." Fang looked across at the promotory which jutted just beyond the glass panels at the edge of the terrace. "I should think we're as close to the rock here as at any point in the castle. And consider All Things Past and Present, the place is right next to where the caves, carved into the rock, emerge from the ground. And in the cave at Matlock Bath, where you attached to Alaysia, we were surrounded by rock."

"I see it, but what's rock got to do with it?"

"All types of rock give off radiation, remember the display in the rock shop at Matlock Bath? Maybe, when you're close to rock, and there's enough of it, the radiation it supplies is sufficient energy to act as one of the elements of reattachment, the push if you like."

"One of the elements?"

"I am thinking that attachment needs a push and a pull. The energy emanating from the rock is the push and something between the person and the spirit is the pull, an affinity or a shared emotional experience, the factor that allowed you to attach to Alaysia and Jasmine to the waiter?"

Fang's logic made sense to me, a push and a pull.

"Fang, the pull, we should at least have an affinity to our own bodies, shouldn't we? All we have to do is get them to one of the locations where matches have happened. And that's why I couldn't attach to my body in the ward at the hospital, it was probably not the right place, too far from the rock. If I only had tried in other parts of the hospital then attachment might have worked."

"I like your optimism and getting our bodies to a place where we know attachments have worked should be our next step, the café would be the best place to try. I have some thoughts on how to get our bodies there, we'll need to use the hotel computer. But remember Fred, we are not the same as those that have matched, our bodies are still alive."

After finding Eliza, back at the forest, and promising to return before the museum closed, Fang and I set off for the hotel. On the way, Fang shared her ideas with her usual enthusiasm, excitedly weaving her way around me as we walked. By the time we reached the hotel the plan to attempt re-attachment had been honed and finalised.

We had decided to lure our bodies to the café by emailing them an invitation to complimentary tea and sandwiches over lunchtime on Thursday. Fang would create a convincing email address from which the invite could be sent from the hotel computer. The invite would make clear that as the café was freely open to the public and that the museum ticket desk could be bypassed. Once our bodies were at the café, Fang and I would, hopefully, be able to re-attach. If attachment did not work then our bodies would be left red-faced, when the invite was revealed to be fake, but otherwise unharmed. Fang's body's invitation was for 12.15 pm, during her lunch hour, and my body's was an hour later. We had decided on different times to minimize the chance of them meeting each other, who knows what would happen if they met and started talking?

Our plan was not perfect, and we had spent considerable time thinking through the permutations of what could go wrong. Our bodies may not even see the email or see it and simply ignore it. And we were only too aware that even if our they did see the email then our bodies might deduce it a scam, however, the realism bestowed by Fang's skills and the use of the castle's livery would minimise any such risk. We also realised that our plan was a one-shot; there was no time for a backup as Fang would have to leave Nottingham with her body on Friday morning.

If only one of us got attached, and assuming they remembered their excursion into the spirit world, then they should at least stay in the café and write notes of anything that they deemed important onto their phone screen so the other could see. Beyond this we had memorised each other's addresses, phone numbers and email addresses for any future attempt at communication. We also swapped some personal details, such as birthdates, feeling that such information could prove useful.

At the hotel, the morning rush had died down and within fifteen minutes of arriving the receptionist, Ivor, who was back on duty that morning, had retired to the back room. We took our chance on the computer and, once again, my finger followed Fang's as we set about our task. Within five minutes a professional-looking invitation had been sent and all traces of our work removed from the laptop. With our business concluded, and relieved the wheels to our reattachment were in motion, we headed back to the castle. It was not long before my mind meandered. Our new understanding had established that spirits in Nottingham were bounded by the rock, yet Fang and I were free to roam. I turned to my friend.

"Fang, any theories on why Eliza and the others can't travel outside the rock." Fang looked at me with pursed lips. "I knew you'd have the answer, what is it?"

"I'm not sure this is an answer but the rock must

sustain spirits by creating some sort of atmosphere. Maybe the radiation that rock emits is the oxygen of the spirit world and away from the rock and there's not enough to sustain a spirit presence. To think and to move then spirits need living souls to think of them, but they need the energy they get from the rock too."

I considered Fang's words, old Nottingham built on its rock, an island of ghosts. How many places where rock emerges from the ground could support a population of spirits: a village built on a gravel ridge or a town nestled in a riverside gorge? What about buildings constructed from stone: ancient castles, medieval abbeys and stately mansions? All could act as cocoons for spirits released throughout the centuries. *Confined to the place where they met their death.*

Back at the museum, we were in for a surprise. Having found Eliza and Jasmine in the forest they immediately turned us around and led us out of the castle grounds. A tour of the city ensued, starting with the Old Lace Market where the landscape had hardly changed in two centuries. Further into the city, the old buildings of Victorian Nottingham had largely given way to the modern architecture of commerce and Eliza was able to describe how things used to be: the indignity of the tenements, the desperation of the ale houses and the tyranny of the mills. That afternoon I saw a Nottingham overlain on top of my own, we even met some of the less illustrious spirits who had adapted to their modern surroundings. Time and terrain move on, but here, in the other Nottingham, the spirits continue to flourish, biding their time with memories of the old places until the city delivers them their match.

CHAPTER TWENTY-NINE

It was mid-afternoon on Wednesday when Fang, Eliza, Jasmine and I reached the row of bus stops outside the hospital ready in our quest to match Eliza and Alaysia. We had reasoned that Alaysia and her grandma would most likely arrive by bus and, in any case, from where we stood there was a good view of the hospital entrance should they arrive by some other means. Moreover, the bus stops were close to the outcrop of rock where the push for reattachment would be as strong as anywhere in the hospital.

With buses coming and going every minute or so, we had taken up position several yards from the display screen to avoid the host of passengers heading for their respective queues. We could, nevertheless, still make out the times of imminent arrivals as they came up on the screen. It was when the timetable information was replaced by a familiar image that my apprehension turned to excitement.

"Look," I said, turning my gaze to Eliza and Jasmine,

"on the screen, an advert for Matlock Bath. That's where we first met Alaysia and where I attached to her. Let's hope this is a good omen." My last sentence froze in the air for fear that I had put a jinx on our afternoon's venture. Then the real significance of the advert struck me. "Fang, do you think this is what sent Alaysia to Matlock Bath?"

"Maybe. If she used these bus stops then she would have seen the advert, Cable cars, gift shops, cafes and amusements for all ages, it sounds enticing enough, doesn't it?" A knowing smile spread across Fang's face.

Another thought struck me, was advertising also the reason why Fang's body had headed for Matlock Bath? I was sure I had seen a leaflet for the place on the desk in her hotel room, a leaflet plucked from the tourist stand in the hotel reception. I mused at my new idea, feeling it tantalisingly close to the truth; had marketing, which sends thousands to the same place, thrown up a chance encounter with Alaysia? It seemed that fate was on our side, and I prayed silently for our good providence to continue.

At just past three o'clock, a bus from the direction of Castle Meadows pulled into the stop and the doors swung open to reveal Alaysia and her grandma. Alaysia hopped off, seemingly untroubled about the medical tests ahead of her, and was followed by her more cautious grandma who gripped the handrail as she alighted.

Eliza stared at her double, no doubt in astonishment, and the four of us went into a hush; the moment had arrived.

Eliza stood in Alaysia's path and closed her eyes. I realised this might be the last time I saw our small spirit friend and blinked back my sorrow.

"Bye Eliza," said Jasmine. I said nothing, rendered silent by my mix of emotions.

As Alaysia passed, Eliza was brushed aside; the match had not worked. Eliza's face did not falter, mine did; In spite of my sentiments, I had hoped that the match would happen, fearing the chances would be no better as we moved away from the outcrop. Jasmine was undeterred, urging Eliza to follow Alaysia and to keep trying. On the approach to the hospital entrance, Eliza got in front of Alaysia, stopped, closed her eyes and was brushed aside again. Alaysia and her grandma passed through the entrance doors and headed down the main corridor, looking up at the multitude of signs as they went. We followed in their trail and it was not long before Alaysia stopped at a branch from the main corridor that led to the prayer room.

"Grandma, the prayer room, can I go and blow the candle out?" she asked.

"We'll go on the way home, I promise," said Alaysia's grandma, turning back to Alaysia. "At the moment, I just want to get us safely to the scanning department, come on sweetheart."

There was no protest from Alaysia, seemingly happy with her grandma's promise and she scurried to catch up. Alaysia's pause had given Eliza another chance to try to match, but once again to no avail. As Alaysia and her grandma had set off again, Jasmine chirped away at her friend, refusing to show any sign of disappointment. At the end of the corridor was a set of stairs that led to the upper floors. Alaysia's grandma grabbed the banister with one hand and Alaysia's hand with the other and they started their climb.

At the third-floor stairwell, a sign indicated that the scanning department was through an adjacent set of double doors. The sign, however, was not the only thing to catch my attention; the chattering between Eliza and Jasmine had stopped. The quiet had not gone unnoticed by Fang either, and we turned together; our two companions were standing motionless about a dozen steps below us with expressions of anxiety.

"We can't go on," said Eliza, "everything is fading."

"Same here, we'll have to turn back," added Jasmine.

Fang and I rushed back and ushered Eliza and Jasmine down the stairs, not stopping until we were back on the ground floor.

"Eliza, are you okay, I mean, what happened?" I asked with a myriad of possibilities running through my mind. Perhaps climbing the stairs had caused Eliza to have a flashback to the mill which was built on this very site, then again why would Jasmine be affected?

"Proximity to the ground," interjected Fang. "By the time we got to the third floor, we must've been over twenty metres from the ground and too far from the bedrock. For Eliza and Jasmine then it would be just like walking outside of the rock. What do you think you two?"

"That's exactly what it was like," replied Eliza.

"I agree," added Jasmine, "we strayed too far from the rock."

The four of us stood in silence. With Alaysia now out of reach and chances of a match looking ever more remote, Eliza's resolve was beginning to crumble, her cheeks hollowed and her eyes fell to the floor. My heart tugged and I looked to Fang for inspiration, she returned a wide smile.

"I have a plan. Fred, go with Eliza and Jasmine to the prayer room, we know Alaysia will return there after her appointment. Eliza, you could try matching again when she arrives. I'll go to the scanning department to find Alaysia and see what I can learn about her condition and when she's likely to be finished. I'll join you as soon as I can."

In the prayer room, the electronic candle flickered away through its rainbow cycle and Fang had been right, there was a sensor, discreetly placed on its stem just beneath the artificial flame. With the place to ourselves, Eliza, Jasmine and I took up position on the front row of seats to admire the abstract angel so cleverly created on the front wall. As our nerves settled, I told them how Fang and I were likely sustained by our living bodies, giving us the ability to travel outside the rock. Within fifteen minutes, Fang had joined us to report that Alaysia's assessment had started with an injection of a dye that would help show more detail on the X-ray scan. Conversations between Alaysia's grandma and the medical staff had revealed nothing about Alaysia's condition other than the procedure was a routine one. After delivering the much-anticipated news, Fang took the seat next to mine, her eyes widening as she looked upon the abstract.

"Wow, this is the angel mural you spoke of, the one Alaysia drew," she said.

The thought that Fang was the angel itself had never left me, and with Fang by my side then I could think of nothing else.

"Yeah, isn't she quite something?" I replied, turning to face my friend.

"Quite something." Fang's simple smile gave no

indication of emotion other than mild appreciation as she scanned the artwork. If Fang was an angel, then she was not going to let on. For my part, I was not going to try and draw an answer any more than I just had.

As we waited, none of us wanted to leave the room, save for the occasional look into the corridor, happy to chat or sit in silent observance when occasional visitors briefly joined us. It was when we heard the approaching sound of light, hurried footsteps that we rose from our seats like a congregation anticipating the arrival of a bride. We turned to see Alaysia at the entrance, looking pleased that the room was seemingly unoccupied. She ran straight to the candle and waited for the colour yellow.

"I wish, I wish..." said Alaysia before closing her eyes, lifting herself on her toes and blowing gently against the sensor beneath the flame. Eliza was already beside Alaysia and blew gently also. My gaze concentrated on the candle, which dutifully extinguished its flame. The darkness lasted a second before the candle relit itself in the most brilliant of white flames. I momentarily squinted then looked to Alaysia, but where was Eliza? Fang and Jasmine were also staring at Alaysia.

"It worked, they matched, they did it." cried Jasmine blinking back emotion.

By this time, Alaysia's grandma had walked through the doorway and approached Alaysia at the candle, which had returned to its cycle of rainbow colours.

"Have you done it?" asked Alaysia's grandma.

"Oh yes, I've done it," replied Alaysia.

"Blow it out again, if you want."

"No thank you, once is quite sufficient. What's for dinner?"

"What would you like, you must be hungry after all that fasting?"

"Fresh bread, please."

Alaysia's grandma laughed, the first time I had seen her do so and a hearty laugh at that. She grabbed the back of a chair with one hand to steady herself as she clutched her chest with the other.

"Oh, Alaysia, you are funny. Just fresh bread?"

"Not just fresh bread, with fish fingers, of course."

"Of course. A fish finger sandwich made with fresh bread - completely perfect."

Alaysia and her grandma boarded the bus for Castle Meadows seemingly none the wiser that they had been shadowed from the prayer room by three spirits, yet there was little doubt from Alaysia's conversation that Eliza was within her thinking. In the matching of Eliza to Alaysia, we had witnessed something momentous, a joining of two halves, a rebirth. I was grateful that Fang and I had been able to help make reparations for Eliza's untimely death; we had redressed a tragedy and it felt like our excursion from humanity had achieved its purpose. Eliza's new life journey had begun and I hoped that Alaysia and Eliza would thrive together, perhaps attachment would help with the medical issue that had brought Alaysia to the hospital. To me, it felt like the end of the story. If I returned to my body then, no matter how strong my feelings were, it would not be appropriate to seek Alaysia out. I silently prayed for a happy outcome and from this point onwards faith was to be my best companion.

CHAPTER THIRTY

With a new day came a new challenge, the attempt to attach Fang and me to our bodies. Lunchtime was approaching, the café chalkboard had been updated with the dish of the day and Fang, Jasmine and I were gathered at the museum entrance.

As we waited in expectation of Fang's body arriving, a state of anxiety had overtaken me. So much hinged on the next few hours and running through the permutations of how matters might unfold was testing my endurance. Our adventures with Eliza had pre-occupied us but now my worries for Lou lashed the forefront of my mind; what amount of upset had my body already caused? If our afternoon's endeavours were successful then I would immediately contact Lou and try to set matters right.

Jasmine chatted away with Fang, and I was glad of it, their words distracted me from my inner turmoil. Jasmine spoke of how Eliza might influence Alaysia to visit the castle and into Jasmine's sphere of influence with the waiter. A seemingly coincidental meeting between the two humans would bring Eliza and Jasmine together again and, surely, the kind words spoken would harbour hidden messages of the two spirits. Jasmine's thoughts intrigued me and my mind meandered across less worrisome territory; a chance meeting of two individuals brought about by kindred spirits deep within them, soul mates somehow finding each other through the inner workings of the spirit world. As unlikely as it sounded, it was, nevertheless, a romantic thought that I liked.

At five past twelve, Fang's body emerged from the tunnel entrance and followed the path towards the museum entrance. The three of us excitedly exchanged glances, Jasmine rising to her toes and clapping; it looked like we had a much-appreciated cheerleader. Fang's body was soon upon us and we followed as she made her way through the museum doors. At the reception desk, Fang's body hovered as she studied her phone. The staff member, unoccupied at that precise moment, looked on, sniffing the air.

"Here goes," said Fang and, gesturing a wave goodbye, walked into her body. The result was that she was simply pushed back, attachment had not worked. "If at first, you don't succeed...I'll try again at the café counter, we know a match worked in that exact place."

Jasmine bounced nervously on her toes and aimed encouraging words at Fang's body, who continued to hover as she tapped away at her phone's screen.

"Come on, hurry up, just go to the café," Jasmine urged.

"Can I help?" said the receptionist, cocking an eyebrow at Fang's body.

"It's okay," she replied with a quick smile. "I've been invited to complimentary tea and sandwiches at the café, I'm just getting the email up to show at the counter."

"Free tea and sandwiches at our café? I've not heard of such a thing, are you sure?"

"Yes, here's the email." And Fang's body turned the screen towards the receptionist.

"Can I take a look?" Fang handed the phone over and after a brief pause, the receptionist let out a small, self-satisfied tut. "I'm afraid you've had a wasted journey; this is a fake." He handed the phone back to Fang's body. "The email address, it's close to ours but there's no dot between 'Nottingham' and 'Castle.' Sorry."

Fang's body seemed drained of energy by the disappointment and dropped her phone languidly into her white cotton bag. With all trace of happiness wiped from her face, she wearily turned towards the exit. My heart dropped. Without warning, a voice rang out from inside the café entrance.

"Fang, wait a minute." It was the waiter from the first Saturday. Fang's body turned around and stopped in surprise as he rushed to her side. The new arrival regarded her warmly. "Nice to see you again, why the short visit?"

Fang's body explained the dilemma at which point the waiter took his apron off.

"Right, you can join me," he said with conviction, "it's still quiet and I'll take my break. I get to eat free as a perk and you are now officially my guest for lunch. If you want a sandwich, I'd recommend coronation chicken but you can have anything you please."

"Coronation chicken sounds perfect and I am very

honoured to be your guest," said Fang's body, her smile restored.

The waiter beamed with pride as he ushered Fang's body in the direction of the café but not before throwing a questioning stare at the receptionist, who stood preening himself, unconcerned by his lack of courtesy. Fang and I followed, soon finding ourselves at the side of the counter next to Fang's body as the waiter explained the circumstances to his colleague, who nodded his understanding. As the waiter disappeared into the kitchen, and in the knowledge that we were at the place where a match had taken place, Fang took her supreme chance and walked into her body but once again just bounced back.

Over the last two days, I had all but forgotten about Fang's warning that we were different to the others, now it took on an immense significance; we were not going to be able to attach in the same way, not in the café and, perhaps, not anywhere else. I was lost for words but Fang's resolute expression told me that she would keep trying. The waiter soon reappeared with a tray loaded with two plates of sandwiches and a pot of tea.

"Let's take the table by the window," he said, tipping his head to point the way.

As Fang's body approached the table, Fang tried to attach again but, once more, she just bounced off. Already resigned to defeat, I turned to my friend.

"It's not going to work, is it? It's like you said we're different to the others, to Eliza and Jasmine." Fang smiled back at me and I sensed that her expectations from the outset had been low enough to temper any sign of disappointment. "For that matter, where is Jasmine?" I asked, looking around the café then back to the reception.

"I'll give you three guesses," replied Fang, as her eyes widened with her gaze fixed upon the waiter. The penny dropped.

"She's attached to the waiter, that's why he came out to the reception, Jasmine's influence. How did you know?"

"He called out my name from the café entrance, my body didn't give her name when they talked on Saturday, so how did he know? When I noticed Jasmine had disappeared, the answer was obvious."

Fang's body and the waiter had started chatting, conversation flowing between them as if they were old friends.

"And thank you for rescuing me out there...I'm so sorry, I don't know your name," said Fang's body.

"It's Vic."

"Thank you, Vic."

"There's nothing to thank me for. It's me who should be thanking you for agreeing to have lunch with me." Vic's crimsoned cheeks were consistent with his heartfelt words.

"Thank you all the same. Being turned away like that was not so nice and would have been a poor memory to end my trip."

"How've you found the UK?"

"I like it but time's gone so quickly. Oh, I have a memento, remember All Things Past and Present, the shop you recommended, look." Fang's body pulled at the collar of her top to reveal the lion's head pendant.

"Wow, I love it. Those red eyes are amazing. Is it gold?"

"It's a type of brass called pinchbeck that's

formulated to look like gold according to the lady who served me, I told her that you'd recommended the place."

"Oh good, was it busy?"

"There wasn't another soul in the place."

"I'll have to keep recommending it. What's it like?"

"You've never been there?"

"I've walked past it plenty of times, but I've never been in."

"But you recommend the place." Fang's body had laughed her words out and as the waiter shrugged his shoulders, she aimed her scrunched lips at him. "You really must pay a visit, find yourself, or a friend, a gift. It's an amazing place. Promise me you'll go."

"I promise, really, I do. Heh, I made chicken rice with fresh ginger root like you suggested."

"You did, how was it?"

"Like a party in the mouth, we should adopt it as our new national dish. I've been recommending it to customers."

As their conversation bubbled along, there was one remark that had caused Fang and I to look at each other in bemusement: *There wasn't another soul in the place*. We had mistaken spirits for customers in the long shop of curiosities.

Having finished their lunch, Vic escorted Fang's body back to the museum entrance where they stood fondly exchanging final farewells. She thanked him one last time and walked towards the tunnel out of the castle grounds. As Vic looked wistfully on, Jasmine emerged from his side.

"Fang," she exclaimed, "you're still here." Fang held up her hands.

"I couldn't attach at the entrance or in the café, though thanks for getting Vic over here. How did you do that?"

"It was easy, I saw him putting the menus out and when it looked like your body was going to be turned away, I went straight over and attached. I suggested he look towards the reception where your body was standing and he noticed her straight away. I felt his heart pound and then he just marched over."

"But how do you attach and detach so easily?"

"I just walk into him and walk out of him."

"There's no magic word?" I interjected.

"No, just that feeling of affinity," replied Jasmine.

"Affinity, I get it, but Fang, why couldn't you attach just now, surely, we have an affinity for our own bodies. Jasmine and the others can attach here, what's so different about us?" The setback had not dented Fang's enthusiasm.

"We need more of a push, more than the rock can provide. It took a burst of energy to detach us, it might take the same for re-attachment; I suggest we start thinking along those lines."

By two o'clock, and having given up on waiting for my body, we headed back into the museum. Not that his absence mattered as we were convinced that attachment would not have worked. And, there was little point in analysing my body's non-appearance, the fact was that Fang and I had run out of time. I now realised that our chances of seeing each other in the future depended on Fang safely boarding the flight to Singapore with her body. Fang was well aware of the peril of the situation too.

"Jasmine, we're going to have to say goodbye," she

said. "My train to London leaves at just past nine tomorrow morning. Fred, we should head back to the hotel to find my body, make sure all is well then wait at the station, whatever happens, I have to get that train with her and we can't risk getting locked in here tonight."

"I'll come to the airport with you," I offered.

"Fred you can't. The journey from St Pancras to Heathrow is partly underground. I will have to follow my body but who knows what could happen to you, the underground stations run deep and you could lose the connection with your body. But come to St Pancras with me. You never know, something might happen on the train. Let's find Clara and Annabella, say our goodbyes and then we need to go."

"Come on then, they'll be in the forest," said Jasmine, her smile faltering. "It's been fun having you around. Fred, if you don't find a way back to your body, you're welcome here."

Jasmine's invitation was gratifying and it should have made me feel better but it did not. Fang would be travelling home and who knows what would be waiting for her in Singapore. And what about Lou, would a return to the castle mean giving up on her?

As we walked through reception Fang's gaze settled on the receptionist who, with no visitors to attend to, was preoccupied with his phone. I still felt aggrieved at the blunt way he had treated Fang's body and his triumphant attitude when he realised the email was fake.

"Annoying, isn't he?" said Fang.

"Totally," replied Jasmine.

"And the way he spoke to my body, as she said, was

not so nice," added Fang. Jasmine and I murmured our agreement. I noticed that Fang was looking at the reception desk laptop.

"Come on Fred, I need you."

With the receptionist just feet away, Fang and I tapped away at the screen, searching through the various computer system options before Fang suddenly straightened up.

"Special concessions," she said, "I think Nottingham's younger generation deserve a little something. "Follow me." My finger followed Fang's and, with Jasmine watching on in wonderment at our earthly abilities, a new message soon appeared in the admissions desk's inbox. The resultant high-pitched ding that resonated from the laptop caught the receptionist's attention.

"Knicky, knocky, ido," announced Fang merrily as he wandered over and read out the title of the message with a raised eyebrow.

"Immediate action required. Free admission for under sixteens from three to six pm today."

By half past three Fang and I returned to the museum reception, ready to set off on our final day of adventuring. Jasmine, Clara and Annabella had joined us – all lured out by the trickle of school children that had reached the forest and which suggested Fang's message might have worked, the hubbub at the entrance confirmed that it had. The queue for entry, mainly comprised of children, snaked around the reception area. The receptionist's tangled hair told of his flustered state and Fang's final flourish had neutralised the sadness of our farewells.

"That's right," said the receptionist to a lady with her three young charges, "free entry for the children. It's an experiment to test the effectiveness of social media according to management. Pass the message on to your contact list, it's an amazing offer. There're your tickets and enjoy your visit. Who's next?"

The train journey to London was uneventful and upon arrival, with Fang having to rush along with her body, dodging the St Pancras crowds, our final farewell was brief. As Fang descended on an escalator into the underground, she turned and simply wished me "au revoir." Despite her final words, I was already fighting off nagging thoughts that I might never see Fang again. With my heart grieving, I was reminded of all the friends that I had lost touch with over the years; was I this casual with my friendships? I promised that should I get back to humanity then I would seek out old friends and draw new friends closer. Above all, I vowed to pick up the courage to tell Lou how I felt about her. Though what chance of telling Lou anything of the sort? I couldn't even say the words in my head.

By the time I had emerged from my web of thoughts, Fang was gone, my memory of her boxed and sealed. Her final words had joined my first, my abiding and my indelible memory of her, the audacious way she had introduced herself to me, *Hi, I'm Fang*. I'd forget my name before I forgot that moment and there was something else about Fang that I wasn't going to be able to forget, my thought that she was an angel.

CHAPTER THIRTY-ONE

I had got in through the front door as my body arrived back at Lou's house late on Friday evening. With no bag, I assumed that he must have returned from the North earlier in the day. With little idea of where he might have been, I did not consciously look for clues. However, an obvious scuff on his right knuckle sent a shiver through me, had he been in some sort of fracas? I dared not analyse the matter further.

My body had sat in front of the television for most of the rest of the night, breaking off only to prepare a snack in the kitchen. I had spent much of the time in the armchair thinking through what my next steps should be, there was little doubt that without Fang then I was a little lost. A trip to the castle to see Jasmine and the spirithood would certainly ease my loneliness, but I was torn, I could not dismiss the notion that Fang might somehow get a message to me and, for that reason, I needed to stay close to my body. Each time he checked his accounts on his phone or laptop then I needed to be there. And so, a visit to the castle would have to wait.

After a night on the settee, I had woken in the most miserable of moods. I had opened my eyes expecting to see Fang but, of course, she was nowhere to be seen and my dozy optimism had inflicted a deeper sense of loss upon me. Being with my body was doing nothing to lift my sense of isolation and, inevitably, my thoughts returned to domestic matters. Lou would be back from her school trip tomorrow afternoon and I was terrified of how my body would behave.

I was interrupted from my angst by a knock at the door, perhaps it was a delivery, something my body had ordered online. I sat upright, there was a shuffling upstairs, he had presumably finished his shower and was now throwing some clothes on. Half a minute after the first knock, there was a second, still my body seemed to be dressing. Then a third and louder knock but why was he not hurrying? The caller might leave, maybe that's what he wanted, maybe it was the police. With my curiosity so obviously going out of control, I moved to the door but could see no one through the opaque tapestry of the patterned glass.

"Hang on," shouted my body as he finally made his way downstairs. He fumbled for the keys in the hall drawer. "I won't be a minute." He opened the door, but no one was there, whoever it was had gone. My body crossed his eyebrows and moved to the step, then squinted in the bright morning sun as he looked down the street. There was no one in sight and no sign of a delivery. He moved back inside and was in the process of closing the door when through the distorting effect of the glass panel loomed a figure, although the outline was indistinct, the vibrant yellow was unmistakable to me.

My body reacted by opening the door again to reveal a familiar figure, complete with shadow, bouncing on her toes. My heart did a forward roll.

"Hi, I'm Fang." My heart did another.

"Hi," replied my body, squinting once more.

"Sorry, I went to try the back door when I heard the front open and came back round. You're Fred?" She had directed the question at my body, seemingly unaware that I was standing right at his side.

"Fang, it's me," I said, but this just confirmed that she could neither see nor hear me. My thoughts raced, Fang must be back in her body and lost the ability to see spirits but, more importantly, remembered our adventures, otherwise how would she have known to come to Lou's? But how had she attached and how was she even here? I had expected Fang to be in Singapore by now. Confused and not knowing what else to do, I circled Fang, half hoping she would sense me from some corner of her eye.

"Do I know you?" said my body, answering Fang's introduction with a questioning stare.

As my worry about Lou transferred to Fang, I realised how courageous she was been. Although we had swapped addresses, our contingency planning had not stretched to the particular set of circumstances that now faced us, though, in the shock, I had quite forgotten the finer details of the plans that we had discussed. I stopped circling and stared at Fang directly, how on earth would she explain matters?

"I'm a friend of a friend, and I need your help."

"My help, of course," replied my body, his demeanour softening under Fang's constant smile. "Your name is Fang?"

"Yes."

"That's a great name by the way, do you want to come in?"

"Sure?" Fang stepped through the threshold and stood in the hallway holding her hands behind her back disarmingly with her white cotton bag over her shoulder. Still smiling, she looked around furtively. It dawned on me she might have anticipated I was here, and for similar reasons that I had circled her, was slowly scanning the surroundings to see if she had retained any ability to see or sense spirits. Her wandering gaze passed through me; the answer was no.

"Come through," said my body and led Fang to the lounge. "You've brought the weather with you, would you like a drink of something, tea?"

At least, my body's small talk showed a friendly disposition. And since such predictable conversation was my own habit when I found myself in a state of anxiety, I surmised his nerves must have been strained by Fang's presence.

"No thanks," answered Fang.

"Take a seat," said my body as he pointed to the armchair while he took up position on the settee, sitting forward and showing keen interest.

"Thank you, this might not take long."

After sitting down, Fang removed her phone from her bag and placed it on her lap with a page of text shining from the screen. Our contingency planning, I remembered, we would write a message for the other. I moved behind the chair and started to read. 'Hi Fred, if you are reading this then place your hand on the back of my neck.' I immediately did what was asked and Fang's shoulders wiggled in reaction, she had sensed me. She made a surreptitious okay sign with her right hand, which I only saw because I was expecting something of the sort in way of acknowledgement. I read on quickly. 'I'm back inside my body, it happened at the airport, I found my push. I need to get your body to an airport. Follow us closely. Wish me luck.'

As the small talk dried up, Fang got down to business and I stood between them wondering how on earth the next few minutes would play out.

"I need to tell you why I'm here; you suffered a lightning strike, is that right?" asked Fang.

"Er, yeah, it struck the ground in front of me, though, rather than hit me, I mean," replied my body.

"Well, I suffered the same thing, lightning struck next to me. For the past two weeks, I've not been myself. How have you been feeling?"

"I have felt a bit different, actually, a lot different, difficulty collecting my thoughts and that type of thing. I can't help but react to whatever is in front of me without thinking, speaking out when I get frustrated by something, so much so that I've managed to get suspended from work, not that I mind. I'm sorry, what was the question again?"

"I was asking how you've been feeling after the lightning strike, you said you had difficulty collecting your thoughts. There is an explanation and your symptoms are quite common. You see, the lightning caused an electrical imbalance and your equilibrium has been disturbed. I have the same symptoms, it's like I've spent the last two weeks in a parallel world." My body had leaned further forward with a ferocious stare. "You're confused?" added Fang.

"You bet I am. How do you know all this stuff?"

"I'm from Singapore and we have lightning there all the time. A lot is known about the effects it has on the human body and our condition is not uncommon. The thing is, there is a therapy that will get us back to normal."

"A therapy?"

"Yes, you know if someone suffers from vertigo then their symptoms can be relieved by judicial movements of the head by a skilled practitioner?"

"I've heard something of the sort."

"With vertigo, they are trying to dislodge rogue crystals that form in the inner ear. Well, it's not an exact analogy, but with our condition, they try and move rogue charges lodged in our minds. Don't worry, there's no electricity involved. The treatment relies on the movement of magnets in a predetermined pattern across the temple." My bodies ferocious stare had softened, and Fang seemed to be on the right lines but where would she go next. "I don't want to go alone to see a therapist, I want you to come with me."

"Where to?"

"Glasgow."

"Glasgow, why of all places Glasgow."

"There aren't many practitioners in the UK, it's still seen as an unconventional treatment here. There is a therapist in Glasgow, with the cheap cost of flights and the airport near here then it's as easy to go there as anywhere else."

Remarkably, Fang's explanation sounded plausible to me, I was glad that I had read Fang's note and knew it was an attempt to get my body to an airport, otherwise, I would have believed magnets placed on the forehead was the answer. But why an airport?

"When are you proposing we go?"

"Our flights are booked for eleven forty this morning from East Midlands Airport."

"Flights? This morning? Fang, you're going too fast." My body paused and blinked his confusion. "Surely you must see how ridiculous all this sounds? The lightning must have affected you more than it did me. Remind me how you know me again, and how do you know I was struck by lightning?" My body's expression had hardened again.

"I heard of your plight from a friend of a friend of yours."

"Who?"

"Nyla."

"Nyla, the amateur phycologist?"

"That's her, Nyla's views on purpose are great aren't they, from pain get gain. That's why I'm here, Nyla thought we could help each other, she had heard from Lou that you had been affected by a lightning strike and when I told her of the treatment that I was planning to have then she was all for it. Please, Fred, I don't want to go alone. If Lou were here then she'd tell you to go with me."

"But Lou's not here..." My body stopped midsentence. He threw his head back, relaxed into the settee and sniffed out a laugh. Looking at Fang with a broad knowing smile, he clasped his hands in excitement. "Fang, you had me going for a second. I mean, I believed you were serious. Lou's behind all this isn't she? I see it clear as day now. A friend of a friend, and bringing Nyla into it was a masterstroke. I don't know what Lou's got planned but she's been rumbled. This is a setup to get me back for the parking ticket, isn't it? I must say, you've played your part brilliantly, you must be one of Lou's old acting friends." There was a pause, my body shook his head. Just as I was thinking all had been lost, he made an announcement. "Right, I'll do it, but only because I want to see what Lou has planned in Glasgow. If she's gone to the trouble of buying tickets there must be something in it, but remember, she's been rumbled."

A car horn sounded outside; my body looked curiously towards the door.

"That'll be the taxi," said Fang. "Get your coat. We're off to the airport, bring some ID." My body froze in astonishment. "Come on, what else is there to do round here."

"Fang," my body protested but I could see, within a couple of minutes, Fang had enchanted my earthly body as easily as she had enchanted his spirit. "All right, I'll get my stuff. Hang on, how long will we be in Glasgow?"

"Not long, we'll travel back tonight, you won't need a bag."

"Right, I'll just use the bathroom and grab my wallet. I'll be two minutes." My body rushed upstairs. Fang looked on with pursed lips. As soon as she heard the bathroom door close, she whispered to me.

"Fred, listen to me carefully. Follow us closely. Outside, I'll keep the taxi door open for you. At airport security, your body will set the metal detector off, and the staff will then give him a full body scan. Be right there with your body and when he gets in the scanner then get in the chamber with him. This is most important. You will notice the scanner has an..."

Before Fang could finish, my body appeared at the top of the stairs.

"I'm ready," he announced.

"Nice hoody," Fang said, as he descended the stairs. My body nipped into the kitchen, returning with a handful of gingernuts and the three of us set off on our new adventure.

CHAPTER THIRTY-TWO

My nerves were in shreds as we walked through the large revolving doors into departures, Fang giving my body instructions all the while.

"Let's take a seat just here," she said, "I've checked us in already, I'll just have to get the boarding passes ready, they're in here somewhere." Fang sat down on a bench, with my body taking the seat next to her, and searched through her bag. "Here they are and this is yours." She handed my body the pass but before he could examine it Fang chivvied him along. "Come on then, let's go." My body duly got up and set off in the direction of security "Hang on, what's that on your trouser leg?" Without giving my body a chance to react, Fang brushed the back of his jeans with her hand. "Just stay still." And in a deft movement, she delicately dropped the lion's head pendant from the antique shop into my body's back pocket before continuing to brush down his leg.

"What was it?"

"Bits of crisps, someone must have spilt them on the

seat." Fang showed my body her fingertips, sure enough, there were fragments of crisps.

"Oh, thanks," he replied without a hint of suspicion.

They were soon in security with their footwear and sundries loaded into trays on the conveyor.

"Your top as well sir," said the security officer to my body, who complied taking off his hoody and placing it alongside his trainers. "Have you removed all metal objects from your person?" My body patted his front trouser pockets.

"Yeah, all good."

"Then stand in the queue and wait until you are called through."

The three of us stood in line in front of the metal detector. After being given the signal, my body walked forward and as he stepped through the arch, the alarm went off. The officer on the other side motioned my body to approach him then, after asking permission, did a pat body search. On finding nothing, he steered my body to the large frame of the second scanner. I guessed that the pendant had evaded detection due to its delicacy.

"Wait over here sir, we need you to do a body scan," said the officer. My body was looking a little bemused. Fang soon appeared, having passed through the metal detector with no problem, and smiled innocently towards him.

The circular doors of the scanner slid open, the occupant stepped out and the officer ushered my body forward. As my body entered the machine, so did I and we found ourselves viewing the outside world through the transparent booth. The glass door slid shut and two vertical pillars started to rotate either side of us. I heard a whoosh and then a blue mist enveloped us. I was pulled towards my body and immediately felt heavy. I could hear a heartbeat and feel breathing; I was back inside my body. The doors of the scanner slid open.

"You can step out now sir," said the guard, "you've something in your back pocket."

"Oh, it's my lucky pendant," I croaked, stumbling from the machine. The guard looked on with narrowed eyes as I cleared my throat. "I forgot it was there, sorry, I always wear it when I fly." I retrieved the pendant and placed it around my neck, taking several attempts to fasten the clasp in my state of unsteadiness. Having noticed my instability, the guard, who was surely trained to pick up on such behaviour, regarded me with new misgiving.

"Are you all right sir, you seem a little giddy?" he said. I hesitated, and as I did so I noticed his eyes were now following my sway. He started to move closer to me and then, to my great relief, Fang appeared between us.

"He's fine," she said, "just a nervous flyer." I straightened myself up, desperately not wanting to appear any more of a security risk than I already had.

"You're with him madam?" Fang beamed at the officer.

"Yes, now come on Fred, collect your things and we'll go and get a coffee, that will steady your nerves."

The officer's expression softened, he seemed to have understood the inference behind Fang's suggestion.

"Flying is the safest form of travel you know. You're more likely to die on a drive to the airport than on a flight from it. Do as your friend says, go and have a coffee and relax."

Fang smiled once more at the guard and ushered me

to the conveyor belt to collect my belongings. Out of earshot of the guard, I turned to my friend.

"Fang, it's me, Fred."

"I know, put your trainers on let's get out of here. There's a bus that will get us to the tram terminus which leaves from just outside arrivals."

Fang offered me a guiding arm and we tottered out of the security area through the duty-free shop and found the one-way turnstile to arrivals. As we left the airport building and made for the bus stop, we had a new experience, everyone was noticing us and moved away from our path; we were no longer spectators but participants. The passers-by stared at us, our joyous expressions, no doubt, sparking their imaginations and all of them reflected our smiles. Welcome back to humanity.

CHAPTER THIRTY-THREE

Outside, a drizzle had started to sweep across the front of the terminal and my human senses stirred into action; I could feel the coolness of a breeze and smell the mustiness of the damp ground. Yet, at heart, I felt like my spiritual self. Fang, likewise. We excitedly compared our states to find that our memories of our time in the spirit world were intact but the events our bodies had endured seemed like vague, distant dreams. Fang moved ahead of me and, in her usual fashion, turned back to gauge my expression. The fluorescence of her cheeks had been replaced with a very human glistening glow.

"Have you worked it out yet?" she asked.

"How we got attached, you mean?" Fang's eyes dipped below her eyebrows, of course, that is what she had meant. "Fang, my mind is as wobbly as my legs but it's obvious that the body scanner was key to it all."

"Can you think why?"

"If the scanner was made from rock, then I would have an answer."

"Mm, think a little deeper." Fang scrunched her lips. My mind really was wobbly. I stared blankly. "Why did you think of rock?"

"Because rock gives off radiation." The penny dropped. "Fang, the scanner, to find concealed items they use X-rays, that's radiation, isn't it?"

"Precisely, a burst of radiation, not the strength of lightning but enough to help us re-attach, the push we needed."

"And when did you work it out?"

"At Heathrow Airport security as my body waited in line for a full body scan after setting the metal detector off. A caution sign on the side of the scanner warned of ionising radiation and reminded me that these types of machines, as you said, use X-rays. The possibilities were clear to me but would a pulse of X-rays be enough of a push? There was only one way to find out."

"What happened?"

"More or less, the same as what happened to you. As soon as my body was ushered into the scanner, I got in with her. As the vertical arms of the machine rotated round, I saw the blue mist and then it seemed like I just disintegrated. As the doors opened, the sudden weight of my limbs was overwhelming, I was attached but could hardly move.

"The guard peered into the scanner and said I could step out. After I stumbled from the machine, the guard said I was free to go, just like that. I thanked him, literally coughing the words out as I learned to use my physical voice again. Without thinking, I caressed my throat and realised what had set the metal detector off."

"What was it?"

"The lion pendant, with it being so light and below

her neckline, my body must've forgotten she was wearing it."

"And you came straight back to find me?"

"Pretty much. After collecting my belongings, I thought I should tell the airline I wouldn't be flying so headed to my gate. I was so off balance by the time I got there that I had to prop myself up against the front desk. The airline official who was hovering round came over and guided me to an assisted boarding seat then radioed a colleague. Help arrived, in the form of a medic and she started asking questions. I didn't tell them of my intention to cancel as I had a feeling about where the conversation was heading. Looking very concerned, she patted me on the back of my hand and said she thought I may have an infection of the inner ear and it was better that I didn't travel though not to worry, I could transfer to the Sunday flight at no extra cost.

"She took me to the airline's lounge and after a respectable period of recuperation, with the help of a freshly roasted coffee, I headed back to find you with my plan to get your body to the airport already hatched. It was late when I reached Nottingham so took a room in a budget hotel close to the station and came straight here this morning. The rest you know."

"And it was nerve-wracking to watch, you must've been terrified. How did you know your plan would work?"

"I really didn't. I had to try something and it was the best plan I had. And here's the thing, as I was thinking the plan through, I wondered what other pieces of equipment might help with reattachment. When my mind reached a hospital scanner, that solved another mystery."

“Another mystery?”

“Eliza matching with Alaysia.”

“But they were never in the scanning department together, Eliza couldn’t get there.”

“Ah, but in preparation for the scan, Alaysia was given an injection of tracer dye, a radioactive substance that produces better images of the inner body. She undoubtedly retained some of this radioactivity when she visited the prayer room. Together with the background radiation, there was enough push for the matching to work. It explains why Eliza couldn’t match to Alaysia in the corridor just down from the prayer room before the scan but could in the room itself afterwards.

“With another piece of the puzzle in place, I felt certain that if I could only get your body to the airport scanner, and you with him, that attachment would work. I was doubly determined and just hoped your body would succumb to the power of suggestion. I must admit, I hadn’t anticipated that he would think it was one of Lou’s tricks and, in the end, I think it was his adoration for her that brought him along.”

“I also think your personality had something to do with it, he seemed a little in awe of you.”

Fang’s cheeks reddened a little, a very earthly reaction. Our return to humanity had certainly interfered with my idea that Fang was somehow an angel manifested from the prayer room. That said, I had more admiration than ever for, what now seemed to be, her mortal abilities. And Fang’s loyalty to me was beyond question, a lump in my throat formed at the thought. Not wanting to get maudlin, I moved the conversation on to mundane matters.

“One question Fang, most important, do you prefer

coffee to tea?"

"Coffee, one hundred per cent. In fact, coffee is just the thing you need to settle your mind, let's go back inside the terminal and get one, it has to be freshly roasted though. We have time before the bus arrives and we should tell the airline we're not flying."

And so, we had our freshly roasted coffee before returning home. Amidst the elation at our return to humanity was a sobering thought, Fang had to travel home the following morning. With so little time left, our attention soon turned to what we should do for the remainder of the day. As both of us had not eaten since breakfast, and it was now heading towards midafternoon, our conversation centred around food. We found that we could not agree on what or where to eat. This was a problem that Lou and I occasionally faced and the solution was to stay at home and cook something. I cautiously suggested chilli con carne and a trip to the local convenience store, the very well-stocked shop as Lou called it as it usually sold those not-so-common ingredients that recipes have a habit of listing.

"You know what," said Fang, "if we're going shopping why not get the ingredients for chicken rice? I could teach you how to make it and you would have another dish to impress your friends."

"Fang, that sounds perfect, I knew you'd have the answer."

And so, the evening went by in the most enjoyable way, the well-stocked shop even had ginger root and Fang proceeded to show me the intricacies of authentic chicken rice and chilli sauce. Fang was most insistent that the ginger root was key, not just for taste but also to aid digestion.

As we ate, inevitably the conversation turned to the future.

"What are you going to do next," asked Fang

"Do you know what," I said, noticing I had picked up some of Fang's phrasing, "I think I am going to go back to college, jobs can wait for a while. I've seen a course here in Nottingham for creative writing with journalism."

Fang suppressed her laughter and took several seconds before she could respond.

"After all you said about journalism?"

"I know, I see the irony, but the journalism bit seems to be bolted on for reasons that elude me, I mean isn't journalism creative writing? In any case, I don't want to move from the area. I want to stay local, here in fact."

"Are you looking forward to seeing Lou?"

"Am I ever, hopefully, I'll be able to smooth things over but what do I tell her about the spirit world?"

"That's up to you."

"What will you do? I mean, will you tell people?"

"I'm going to say nothing, but don't let me influence you. The things that have happened are too fantastic to be true. Even now, part of me is believing it never happened and once I'm back in Singapore, well, it will seem like a dream. I want to return to the UK though, maybe work will bring me back. I'm getting used to the place and do you know what, I'd like to see more museums, more antique shops and more castles. Odd really, an interest in the past."

Our conversation drifted on to more routine matters and we talked until neither of us had the energy to continue. It was ten o'clock and conscious of the early start, we turned in. I soon fell into a deep sleep, surprising given the tumultuous events of the day, perhaps the soothing effects of the ginger were responsible.

Sunday morning arrived and Fang insisted that she travel to the airport alone, with the concession that we walked together to the local railway station. As we made our way over the crossing to the London platform, the significance of the spot hit me once again and I pointed to the repair in the road.

"Fang, that's the patch of tarmac I told you about, the spot where the lightning struck. Isn't it fitting that things should end where they started?"

"Quite fitting," replied Fang, "though I don't think things here have finished yet."

"What do you mean?"

"You'll see. Come along, there're people already waiting on the platform; the train won't be long."

We chatted inconsequentially right up until the express to London drew to a halt in front of us. As Fang boarded, she turned to face me, her expression flat, neither a smile nor a frown.

"Goodbye Fred. Don't stop watching the clouds."

"I won't. Goodbye, Fang." Feeling a rush of sadness, I instinctively clawed at my collar line and sensed the lion's head pendant. I'd completely forgotten it was there. I retrieved the charm and held it between my thumb and forefinger. "Fang, you're pendant." I tried to undo the clasp but with cold, hurrying hands, made little progress. Fang smiled.

"It's okay, you keep it."

"I couldn't, I mean it's your souvenir." Fang waved away my appeal.

"I tell you what, give it to Lou as a gift, it's for a lady

after all, you two have more in common than you think. I'm sure she'll love it. I have to go. There's no need to wait for me to get seated. I'll be in touch." And with that, Fang closed the train door and disappeared into the confines of the carriage. Just as the train started to pull away, the clasp sprang open and I collected the pendant in the palm of my hand. I gazed upon that tiny trinket, bought with little more than a child's pocket money, which meant more to me now than anything else I owned. Fang had been quite perceptive, there was only one person I would ever have passed it to.

With the train out of sight, I started my journey home only to realise that I had meant to ask Fang if she had any last thoughts about a link between Eliza's portrait and myself. Typical that I should remember this after we had parted. Perhaps, there was no link. Regardless, a more pressing question came to mind. How did matters lie between me and Lou? I trembled at the thought.

CHAPTER THIRTY-FOUR

At home, I busied myself tidying the house and cleaning. I'd also set the bread maker off to let its pleasing scent permeate the downstairs rooms. All this activity was aimed at making the house as welcoming as possible for Lou and yet none of it dispelled my trepidation. Was my relationship with her already ruined? I could only wait to find out. Moreover, should I tell Lou about my spirit adventure? Fang had decided she was going to keep the whole fantastic episode secret. I kind of felt the same, who would believe us anyway and if I said anything about Alaysia, what consequences would it have for her? But should I at least confide in Lou? When I had started cleaning, I was sure I would tell her but as the afternoon drew on, I changed my mind. I would say nothing, she would only think me deranged or see it as another joke, a potentially unsettling one and I could not risk any further upset.

And what of the pendant? I was determined to carry out Fang's suggestion to give it to Lou but there was a problem. Why should I get Lou an antique pendant out of the blue? I could save it until Christmas, then again, what's wrong with giving a present spontaneously, especially to someone you admire? Perhaps it was me, perhaps I did not want to show any feelings, or perhaps it would be a creepy thing to do and come across as presumptuous. I scolded myself, how could I tie myself in knots over giving a gift? I wondered what Fang would say about the matter. She would tell me to be bold. And she would not look at it as a problem, she would see it as an opportunity. I decided there and then, I'd give Lou the pendant as a welcome home present and think of some accompanying words by the time she arrived.

It was quarter past four when Lou collapsed through the door, dropping her bags on the hall floor. I had heard the car pull onto the drive so was ready at the door to help her through.

"Lou, how was it? You look exhausted," I said.

"That's exactly how it was, exhausting," she replied, "the kids were hyperactive from the moment they got on the coach to the moment they got off. The accommodation was freezing, my bed was lumpy and the food was mediocre. I'm glad it's over, I'm volunteered out. You've put a loaf on; I love that smell."

"Oh yeah, I thought you'd be pleased. I've boiled the kettle."

"Nice. Oh, I have a present for you. Hang on a minute." Lou pulled a small paper bag from her rucksack and ushered me into the kitchen. She seemed pleased to see me and there was no sign of the animosity that I had feared, my heart was doing somersaults. "I thought of getting you something from one of the French towns we visited but I didn't have a moment to myself to look. I'd given up hope of getting anything but while waiting for our flight at the airport there was a small bookshop and I found this." Lou handed me the bag from which I retrieved a book, a collection of short stories to relieve stress and soothe the mind. "You seemed a little stressed before I left, this seemed just the thing."

"Thanks, Lou, that's really thoughtful, I love it. And I've got to admit that I was a bit stressed; I think it was a combination of work and that lightning business."

"You're looking much better than the last time I saw you. I thought you were having some sort of breakdown; it was obvious you weren't yourself. And I still don't understand why they released you from the hospital in that state. I still think I should have taken you back but you were dead against it; do you remember?"

I nodded, though it was news to me, and sensed that Lou's suggestion to take me back to the hospital had caused my body's outburst which I had witnessed with such terror. "I'm glad I texted you to suggest a trip to your parents. I wasn't trying to get rid of you by the way, I just thought a visit to your folks would do you, and them, good."

"I'm sure it did, and I may call the surgery tomorrow, I feel fine, but just as a check."

Lou beamed.

"And I'm going to get Nyla around here, I'm sure she'll have a theory on all of this. I bet you had some sort of mental trauma due to the strike; it must have been terrifying."

"Yeah, get Nyla round, I've loads of questions for her. I could cook."

"Omelette or chilli con carne?"

"Neither, chicken rice."

"Chicken rice?" Lou laughed the words out.

"Yeah, the national dish of Singapore."

"Gosh, is this new interest in cuisine a result of the lightning strike?"

"Erm, sort of."

"Okay, it's a deal, I'll ask if she can make it next Friday."

Our conversation had been warm and it felt an ideal time to reciprocate Lou's gift.

"I've got you something too, call it a welcome home present." I retrieved the pendant from my wallet and handed it to Lou, who stared at the gift with raised eyebrows. I wished that I could have read her thoughts and, anticipating a potentially awkward silence, continued my narrative. "You see, I was wandering around town and found myself in the antique shop, the one just outside the shopping centre. The charm is made from an alloy that was formulated to look like gold and called pinchbeck, a mix of copper and zinc. I remembered your nickel allergy and thought this would be okay. The alloy dates the pendant to around the early nineteenth century."

While I spoke, Lou had been examining the pendant, weighing it up in her hand while staring at the lion's face. She squeezed the lion's head between the thumb and forefinger of her left hand and flicked the side of the lion's mane with the thumbnail of her right. The lion's head flipped open to reveal a cavity.

"Wow, it's a locket," I exclaimed.

"Of course, what did you think it was?"

"Well, a pendant. I realised it seemed light but thought that was due to the alloy. You knew it was a locket?"

"Of course, and look." I peered into the interior, fixed in place by a tiny yellow bow were curls of copper-red hair. "Fred, this is weird."

"Lou, I'm shocked. I had no idea it was a locket. This isn't a joke." My heart sank, I could not think straight, just as I suspected my gift was backfiring. Lou saw my look of dismay.

"I mean weird in a good way. I love it, and I love a good mystery. I wonder whose lock of hair it was and why it was put in there." Lou closed the locket up. "I'll do some research, see what I can find out but for now I'm ready for a cup of tea?"

In the eventuality, I stuck to my decision not to tell Lou about my out-of-body experience, it just seemed too fantastic. Fang contacted me to say that she had arrived home safely and after a flurry of texts our messages to each other dried up. In time, our spirit adventure started to feel like a dream, just as Fang had predicted. Lou and I agreed on a truce on practical jokes though Lou did warn me that the next time I put my gardening shoes on then to expect a surprise. We were closer than ever and time seemed to fly by. I enrolled on the writing course, with journalism bolted on, and Lou was more than happy to accommodate a student. On occasion, when in need of inspiration with some of my academic assignments, I visited the castle museum. I would have freshly roasted coffee in the café with my notebook poised and, on several occasions, Vic had asked what I was writing about before making a suggestion; I had more than a feeling that it was Jasmine who was forthcoming.

One Sunday morning in early October, Lou and I had

walked out, arms linked, after I had suggested a stroll around the nature reserve. We repeated the route that I had taken on the night of the lightning strike with the same result on the way home - the barrier to the railway crossing came down in front of us. I laughed at the thought of it, what a change since that fateful night, how my life had transformed for the better. As the train passed slowly in front of us, I stared up at the windows and thought of Fang. So strong was the feeling that she was about to appear from behind me that I looked over my shoulder expecting to see her familiar figure. I recalled my fanciful thought that she was an angel who I had called from the hospital prayer room, a thought that had never left me. I was beyond grateful to Fang; my happiness was in no small part due to her. I was more than happy; my prayers had been answered. And together we had done something extraordinary, helped Alaysia and Eliza match. But why me and why Fang and what were the links between us all?

My mind switched back to Fang, I remembered her understanding of my emotions, her unusual intelligence, her optimism and her smile, all of which had carried me along in her coattails. She was a force of nature, by my side and on my side as we steered a safe passage through our adventures. At that moment, an astonishing thought flashed across my mind. Other thoughts readily threw themselves forward and they all pointed in the same tantalising direction. Fang had described herself as a problem solver for a customer in the UK. Was I the problem customer? Had Fang arrived to help me? My idea that Fang was an angel had resurrected itself but with a modification; Fang was not just an angel – she was my guardian angel.

"Fred, are you okay?" asked Lou. I had been so self-absorbed that the barrier had risen without me noticing.

"Yeah, perfect," I replied instinctively. Yet I was almost stuck to the spot as my astonishing conclusion settled upon me. I glanced across at Lou, whose round, inquisitive eyes were fixed on mine.

"Then why are you moving so slowly?" Lou had been tugging at my arm to encourage me along but only managed to move me a couple of yards due to my thought-induced inertia. She turned to face me and moved closer; we were now toe to toe. I caught a glance of the lion's head locket, which Lou had taken to wearing, gleaming gold in the morning light.

I heard Fang's voice.

Be brave. Tell her.

I felt the hairs on the back of my neck rise.

Fred, Tell her, now.

"The thing is, Lou, how can I say this? The thing is..." I closed my eyes. "I love you."

I opened my eyes. It was as if Lou had been expecting to hear my words, she moved closer still and kissed me quickly on the lips. It was as if lightning had struck again, but the flashes and feeling of flying through the air were metaphorical. "I know. Now, should we go or should we stay here and get run over by the next train?"

I looked down at my feet, we were standing right on top of the fresh tarmac where the lightning had struck.

"Stay here, it seems to be my lucky spot." We kissed again, more lightning. I remembered Fang's words.

I don't think things here have finished yet...You'll see.

And I did see. Fang, my glorious guardian angel, had never left me.

CHAPTER THIRTY-FIVE

It was a few weeks into the school term after the new year and Lou had arrived home a little late but full of enthusiasm. I had expected as much, on both counts, as it had been the day that she started casting for the school play. Lou had spent a good part of the festive break modifying scripts at the kitchen table. She had been so taken with the locket and thoughts of its mysterious past that she had written it into the play.

Lou had mused on who might have owned the locket and why the hair was placed inside of it, but after a little research had decided such things were best kept as a mystery, saying that it was enough that the locket was now in safe hands and cherished by someone who appreciated its secrets.

The subplot that Lou had come up with was along the lines of finding Cinderella from a glass slipper, the hair in the locket needed to be matched with a person from a futuristic city. The way Lou had weaved the new additions into the storyline was, I thought, very inventive.

Lou joined me in the kitchen where I was consulting one of my textbooks over a cup of tea.

"How did the casting go?" I asked, in my surety that her state of excitement related to her extracurricular activity.

"Brilliantly, I cannot tell you how good it was," she replied.

"Why, what happened?"

"I found the perfect person as a match for the locket, and I mean perfect."

With my interest stirred, I looked up from my book.

"Tell me more?"

"When I started, my idea was that I would cast the person to be paired with the locket and just pretend the colour of the hair in the locket matched theirs, but my favourite for the part was a girl with red hair of the same shades. She was a natural and said her lines perfectly. She lived the words I gave her and I was left feeling a little overwhelmed. She's my girl and could go a long way with the right direction. She just started at the school last September and I'm going to keep her under my wing, that's for sure."

I put my book down with goosebumps rising.

"What's she called, this new star?"

"She's called Alaysia."

I had not thought of it until now but the Alaysia I had known, being around ten when I met her, would be the right age to have recently started at senior school and was in the catchment area of Lou's academy.

"Alaysia, that's a great name. Do you have a photo?"

"Why yes." And Lou retrieved her phone from her bag, scrolled through a few images then held out the screen. "Look, here she is with the locket."

Sure enough, shining back from the screen, with a dimpled smile and showing off the locket in her outstretched hands, was Alaysia looking healthier than ever. I fought back tears.

Heat rose through me; my face flushed. It had not escaped my notice that the hair in the locket was similar in colour to Alaysia's, and I knew enough about lockets, courtesy of Lou's research, that they were sometimes used as mourning jewellery. Moreover, the age of the piece matched the time of Eliza's death. I remembered the strands of hair kept by her mother and the few trinkets of cherished jewellery taken by the local trader; was the locket, with Eliza's hair secured within, among them? It would certainly have been the perfect way, along with the portrait, to preserve Eliza's memory. Was this my mind running wild again? Were all these events coincidental? I remembered Fang's words, about coincidences hiding unexpected truths. Much as I tried to deflect my thoughts, they were all heading to one inevitable conclusion. The hair in the locket was Eliza's.

My tightened throat prevented me from speaking. I placed my palm instinctively across my heart and turned to Lou who had opened the locket and was staring at the hair, which had not lost its lustre through age, shades of copper, bronze and gold glinting in the brightness bestowed by the fluorescent lights.

"Fred, I keep getting a sense of deja-vu."

I remembered more of Fang's words, that there was a link to find after I had sensed something at the sight of Eliza's portrait. What was Lou sensing? What was the link?

Looking across at Lou, I was noticing the copper fleck

in her hair more than usual. And Lou had referred to Alaysia as 'my girl.' My imagination has so often run away with me, obscuring true north and leading me to erroneous conclusions that I tried to stop my mind from racing away, but I was already piecing together fragments. My mind raced on with thoughts snowballing, each one enveloping the previous. Parallel after parallel all supporting the same supposition without exception. Lou's love of fresh bread reminded me of Eliza's mother. Lou's imagination, creating plots for the school play, matched with Eliza's mother's habit of making up bedtime stories. Lou's hatred of fast fashion sweatshops - was this some inherited emotional trauma from a nineteenth-century cotton mill? And the way Lou had instinctively opened the locket the first time she had seen it as if she had opened it a hundred times before. My heart pounded as my mind reached its incredible conclusion; Lou had been Eliza's mother in a life that had passed long ago. And, reunited through Alaysia and Lou, Eliza and her mother had finally found each other.

Lou placed her hand on mine. Tears had welled in her eyes, though the smile on her face told me that these weren't tears of sadness but tears of contentment. And knowing Lou, when she said she would take Alaysia under her wing she meant it in no uncertain terms. Now I had a link between Lou and Eliza's portrait but still the link between me and the portrait remained a mystery. My affinity for Alaysia, my affinity for Lou and now Lou's affinity for Alaysia, what was this triangle forming between us?

And in that moment, my desperate loss of words, a trait that had blighted me all my life, gave its dividend, for it was a trait which matched me to Eliza's father. And my feeling of protectiveness towards Eliza's portrait, I could not precisely explain it at the time but the feeling a father would have for his daughter would fit the bill entirely. My unexpected outburst of anger at the sight of Cromford Mills – did I have an element of inherited emotional trauma too? But these were such slender connections for such a momentous supposition. My emotions, however, were far from slender, and the conclusion my mind had so readily just raced to would not be diminished. Finally, and blessedly, the link between me and Eliza, I had been her father in times past. My heart lit up like I'd emerged from a cold, dark, damp tenement room into a bright midday sun, a hundred thousand midday suns. I basked in the wonder of my realisation and found Lou was not the only one with moistened eyes.

Finally, the detail that made sense of everything, the link between me and Eliza, the reason I had sensed something at the sight of her portrait. The reason I had been spirited from my body. And when I had prayed for help, who else but my guardian angel would have appeared by my side? The very angel who guided me to the portrait and put me right in front of Alaysia. All other questions and curiosities fell away; angels have their ways.

Lou and I were looking upon the locket as if two proud parents, surely that is exactly what we had been. Was now the better times and the hereafter, and what possibilities for this extraordinary girl Alaysia? Go, Alaysia, go.

ABOUT THE AUTHOR

Martin Tuffs was born in Teesside and after gaining a PhD in Materials at Leeds University moved to the East Midlands where he worked as a Materials Engineer in the aerospace industry for over twenty-five years.

He resides in Nottingham with his wife, two children and one Cocker Spaniel. Martin has now turned his attention to creative writing. His first novel, 'Out of Humanity,' was written as an uplifting tale of the supernatural with elements of mystery and romance.

Find him at **www.martintuffs.com** and on **Instagram**

Printed in Great Britain
by Amazon

32813043R00152